# LET IT BE AT THAT

# LET IT BE AT THAT

BOB ALLEN

Purpletooth Publishing

# CONTENTS

Dedicated to my best friend and rock, my wife Laura.

# CHAPTER 1

# THE DAY AFTER CHRISTMAS 1969

In a cool way, Gary "Weezer" O'Donnell did not feel like he felt he should feel. The day after Christmas was usually the day that you show off the presents that you were given the day before. But this year, Weezer just wasn't feeling it. The holiday to him had become a routine celebration of the practical. A dress shirt from Aunt Rita, new pajamas from Mom and wool socks from Dad. The only thing he enjoyed now were the days off from school, which allowed him to hang out all day at his current destination, the flooded parking lot turned skating rink behind the VFW hall on 69th and Honore.

But not all his Christmas presents were duds. His older brother Tim gave him the new CCR album, "Green River." He would put his headphones on and sink into it later over the weekend. Earlier that year, Weezer decided that albums were cool and made a serious life decision that he would only buy albums from now on. He now had four. The *"Green River"* album, the Who's *"Tommy,"* Led Zeppelin II and the soundtrack from the film "Mary Poppins." He had somehow inherited the double album from his mother. He never played it but thought the double-record jacket added a visual heft to his collection, so it stayed among the other albums, hefty but unplayed. Weezer felt that his days of buying forty-five singles were long gone.

God, I'm cool.

It was true, however, that he was currently wearing the wool socks that his father had given him, but he wasn't trying to show off or display anything. First off, the socks were practical for skating and second, you can't even see the damn things when you had on your shoes or skates.

What was even cooler, he felt, was that for the first time in his life, Weezer had to be woken up on Christmas morning. Just a little after ten o'clock, his mother peeked her head into his bedroom and said "Gary, it's Christmas morning. Get your ass out of bed." In the past, he would stir early, waiting like a feral nocturnal predator for the first hint of movement from another member of the house and once he heard the movement, usually his mother in the kitchen starting the coffee, he would spring up like a rabid, greedy child and sack the front room, attacking any present that had his name on it. A riot of torn wrapping paper and Weezer playing with one of his opened gifts would await the rest of the family when they entered the front room. There were far more gifts under the tree then, as both of his older brothers, Tim and Greg, were still living at home and actively participated in the Christmas morning exuberance with a bilateral truce between them. They were classic Irish twins who had the standard brother issues of the time and either of them could lay a barrage of verbal assaults on the other at the drop of a hat. However, they both displayed an almost mature aspect to their relationship on this one morning and it added something special to the occasion. To Weezer, the rare experience was a large part of his anticipation. He liked to see his brothers in this mood. It made him feel good.

Weezer finally complied with his mother's wish, rose from bed, put on his robe, and met up with the family in the front room where his father would pass out the presents to the three of them, one by one.

The small tree was lightless and had the usual O'Donnell family ornaments dangling precariously on the now sagging and brittle branches. Weezer's father had gotten the tree from Fat Billy as payment for a day of labor at Billy's tree lot on 71st and Damen. He had spent an entire afternoon at the lot, ostensibly to help Billy sell his trees, but he ended up most of the time standing next to Billy and a garbage can full of fire, drinking beer and shots of Hiram Walker. He came home that evening smelling as if he spent the day in a burning tavern, with the tree that Fat Billy had given him as payment for his labor. He raved continuously about the tree as he dragged it into the front room and said that he thought it was the most beautiful tree he had ever seen. He awkwardly put it in the tree stand and positioned it as best he could in front of the windows. He moved the Gold Star Banner one window over, so it would still be visible while the tree was up. He stepped back and, with a glow of almost spiritual reverence, started to weep.

"It's so beautiful, it doesn't even need lights," said Weezer's father.

* * * * * * *

"Wow Dad," said Weezer. "Socks! How did you know?" Weezer knew full well that his father had no idea what he had given him. His mother did all the shopping.

"I'm glad you like them, Gary," said Weezer's father.

"I'll wear them tomorrow," said Weezer with a hint of forced enthusiasm.

Weezer's father nodded, raised his fisted hand to cover his mouth and let out a deep phlegmy cough while he grabbed a Camel from the pack sitting on the small table next to his overstuffed chair. When he finished clearing his lungs, he lit the Camel and grabbed another present.

"To Mom, from Santa," he said in a raspy voice through the smoke he was exhaling. He handed the present to Weezer's mother.

"Me?" said Weezer's mother, in what Weezer thought qualified as mock surprise, as she accepted the gift from her husband.

She unwrapped the gift which revealed a red holiday Wieboldt's box that contained a brand spanking new pink colored terry-cloth house coat.

"Oh my. This is beautiful!" she exclaimed as she stood up from the couch and held the robe in front of her.

"Looks like a perfect fit. Thank you dear," she said as she blew a kiss to her husband.

Having felt that he had successfully accomplished his sole responsibility of the holiday season, other than the tree, Weezer's father smiled back at his wife and took a large congratulatory sip of his coffee and a drag from his Camel.

* * * * * * * *

It was late morning the day after Christmas. Weezer met up with Mike Raskins, his best friend, and Mike's little brother, Kevin, to play ice hockey. It was a bright, cloudless, sunny winter day where low wind and a slight melt of the snow they received the week before forged together to form the perfect weather for an all-day outdoor hockey marathon.

Weezer and Mike walked with their hockey sticks over their right shoulders and their skates, tied together by the shoestrings, hanging over their left. They each had on shin guards, kept in place by large heavy wool hockey socks in the colors of their favorite team, the Chicago Black Hawks. Kevin, meanwhile, who was considerably smaller than his older brother and Weezer, struggled to keep up while wearing new hockey gear that he would grow into.

"So, how was your Christmas?" asked Weezer.

"Pretty cool. Got some new skates. CCMs," said Mike while pointing over his left shoulder. "Breaking them in this morning. Probably have some blisters tomorrow. Kevin got new shin guards, a new stick, and a Hawks jersey. The kid made out like a bandit. How about you?"

"I got some socks," Weezer intoned. "But they're nice socks. Skating socks. I've got them on now, want to see?"

"No, no. I believe you," said Mike.

Kevin entered the conversation. "Yeah, fucking Santa brought me almost everything I asked for in my letter."

Mike looked at Weezer with raised eyebrows that silently said "Yeah, he still believes."

Weezer nodded and chuckled. "Alright, alright," he said to Mike's alarmed eyes.

The trio continued down the block to the corner double lot where Old Mr. Teller lived alone, in a large, dated two-story frame house where he raised a family of four boys with his wife, who passed away about two years ago. The graying house had seen it's better days as Mr. Teller's only concern since she passed, was for the well-being of the five large dogs that lived with him.

The dogs were out today in the muddy yard when they noticed the trio. They immediately ran to confront them but were prevented by a chain-link fence. Kevin screamed as the dog's loud and glistening teeth made their presence known behind what Weezer and Mike knew was an insurmountable barrier. In a panic, Kevin started to run, but with all the over-sized equipment, he had zero agility and promptly fell on his face. Again, he screamed, but this time in pain rather than fear.

"You little pussy," said Weezer.

Mike walked over to his brother as the dogs became more animated and louder.

"C'mon. Get up. You're okay."

Kevin got up and after a few sniffles, he put his knit cap back on, picked up his stick and followed Mike and Weezer.

"Weezer, you suck," said Kevin.

Weezer looked over his shoulder and smiled.

"Just be cool," he said with a laugh.

The rink, for lack of a better term, was the parking lot of the 69th Street VFW Hall. When the cold weather arrived, the fire department would connect hoses to the nearby hydrant and flood the lot and occasionally top it off when they had the time. After a snowfall, the skaters themselves would shovel the ice for their use, which was not really shoveling, but a pushing of the snow to the side to form the parameters of the rink.

When the sun came out, the top layer of the ice would turn into a watery slush that became an essential source of drinking water for the players. Some would take handfuls of melting snow and stick it in their mouths. This method had officially become safe since the Russians ceased their testing of the atomic bomb in the atmosphere, which, as everybody knew, had been contaminating the snowfall in prior years. Small pools of icy-cold water formed on top of the ice, just enough for a good drink. The players would lay flat on their stomachs and place their lips close to the ice and just suck in the water. Today was just such a day, there would be lots of top-melt.

It was still Christmas vacation, so a lot of the skaters wore their Christmas gifts that morning. New skates, new hockey equipment, new coats, hats, and gloves were utilized for the first time in their product lifespan. The rink was crowded, not just with the hockey players. Girls were out wearing their white figure skates with the brightly colored knitted balls attached, trying to make circles or jumps or somehow imitate what Peggy Fleming accomplished in the past Winter Olympics.

The boys arrived and approached the regular group of players in a clear area at the corner of the rink, closest to 69th Street. Bullethead and his little brother Sam, Billy Duffy, Pat Gibbons and Mickey Doty were warming up for the pick-up game that was about to start. Weezer and Mike gave a quick wave to the group on the ice while they sat on a make-shift bench placed against the wall of the VFW Hall to change into their skates. Weezer and Mike accomplished the task in quick fashion. About halfway through his first practice lap around the ice, Mike heard Kevin's plea from the bench.

"Mike! Come help me!"

Mike skated to Kevin.

"I can't get this skate on. Fucking help me, would ya?"

"Calm down spaz," said Mike as he knelt to one knee and held the skate while Kevin successfully crammed his foot into it.

"Now make sure you lace them tight, or you'll just have to keep doing it."

Kevin impatiently nodded while Mike skated away to the center of the ice where teams were already being picked.

Mike, Kevin and Billy Duffy would skate against Bullethead, Sam and Weezer. These were the teams for now. More players would show up during the day to fill out the maximum of four skaters per side, which was the most that their rink could accommodate while still having a decent game.

Pat Gibbons and Mickey Doty were the opposing goalies. Pat had an agility that allowed him to throw his body around, wearing no protective equipment, to stop opposing shots. He also had a thick skull, which is an asset at the position. Pat would regularly take shots off his noggin with no effects, other than an occasional red welt on his face. Once he bled from a scalp wound under his hair. It bled for a bit and streaked down the side of his cheek and neck which Pat thought was cool, so he didn't wipe it away. The wound eventually stopped bleeding and left him with an ugly patch of blood-caked frozen hair on the side of his head. He wore it like a badge and since then, no one has ever questioned Pat's status as a goalie.

Mickey Doty proclaimed himself goalie on the sole basis that he had received a goalie mask for Christmas. Also, he could not skate that well. He was embarrassed that he could only skate while wearing figure skates. Wearing figure skates to a neighborhood hockey game was like wearing a tutu to a football game. It just ain't done. He knew that he could not possibly endure the brutal trash talk that would be directed towards him if he wore his figure skates.

Instead, he would endure a lesser category of pussification by playing while wearing his buckle snow boots. At least while in goal, there is actual risk of physical harm befalling him, so any trash talk directed his way was soft and occasional. He stuffed rags and old towels inside the boots around his ankles as protection and wore a second layer of pants which would act as both shin guards and thigh pads. The neighborhood players let the boot wearing pass, but occasionally someone north of 69th Street would come to play and immediately question the right of Doty to play in snow boots. Any issues were avoided by an aside to the outsider, "Wait until you see him play." His skills were in fact so awful that whenever one team got more than a five-goal lead, they traded goalies. They called it the Doty Rule.

Doty and Gibbons skated, or in Doty's case shuffled, to opposite ends of the rink where each of them set up a pair of weighted coffee cans to form the 'goal' mouth that they would each try to protect from the opposing team's shooters. Behind Doty's goal was 69th Street, a busy thoroughfare on which a steady stream of buses, cars and trucks passed by. Neither of the goals had nets and the rink did not have any boards to stop pucks other than a six-inch bank of snow, which was designed more to define the rink than to stop any shots. With the possibility of financial responsibility for damage to any moving vehicle on 69th Street looming over the events, each game started with all the participating players skating to the center ice and in unison say,

"No chips, no dibs."

This was neighborhood common law. By stating, "no chips, no dibs" before any event, whether sporting, social, criminal, or other, the declarer is immune from any financial responsibility that stems from another individual's act during the mutual participation of said event. So, in other words, you break it, you pay for it.

After the loud anthem-like disclaimer, the teams went to their positions and the game started.

The opening pace was slow as the skaters got familiar with the makeshift rink. The ice surface changed from day to day, depending on the weather. For example, a short melt and then an overnight freeze will leave a nice skating surface but that was not the weather situation today. The past three days had been cold. With all the children on school holiday, the rink had been used extensively and the ice reflected the additional wear and tear. Pocket holes, chips and fissures dotted the ice, lying in wait for the unsuspecting player to have his skate blade get caught and get upended while on a high speed two-on-one breakaway, the result of which ends in hilarious laughter and angry cursing.

After a couple of lazy lobs at each of the goalies, the game's pace picked up. Kevin Raskins brought the puck up from his goal line and approached center ice. He skated around Bullethead's little brother, Sam, with no trouble. In fact, Sam fell while attempting to stay with Kevin, which Kevin noted.

"You ain't shit Sam!"

Kevin had a straight lane for the goal that Mickey Doty was protecting. He flipped a soft bouncing shot that easily got past Doty. Kevin raised his stick in jubilation and yelled, "Yeah!"

He continued crowing as he skated back to his defensive position, "Yeah, baby! Doty, you ain't nothin! I got your ass!"

Weezer retrieved the puck from behind the goal and prepared to lead his team's rush. He turned to Doty.

"You gotta pick it up Doty."

"Yeah, yeah. The little bastard got lucky, that's all," replied Doty.

The game continued at a faster pace. Gibbons was excellent in goal as his team took a five to one lead. Mike took the puck from his own zone and attempted to drive on Doty with Weezer draped all over him. Kevin came from out of nowhere and used his little body as a screen on Weezer, which caused Mike to break away and skate in on Doty for another easy goal.

"Doty, you suck!" said Kevin from center ice.

Weezer skated up to Mike and pointed to Kevin.

"He sure is mouthy today."

Mike gave Weezer the 'what are you going to do?' look and skated off.

Weezer took the puck out and got deep in the opposition zone and was defensively picked up by Kevin. Weezer imagined that he was Bobby Hull, speedily whizzing by an opposing defenseman, holding the puck on the stick with his right hand and using his left arm to keep the smaller boy at bay, or so he thought until he tumbled on the shiny, hard surface when his skate got caught in a large rut. Kevin corralled the loose puck and started back the other way.

"You little shit," said Weezer to himself as he rose and chased Kevin. He gave him a hard hip-check, which sent Kevin sliding, flat on his stomach like an out-of-control pinwheel, into the snow embankment that formed the boundaries of the rink.

Mike skated up to Weezer, "Hey Dickhead!" he said. "He's half your size, man."

"Hey, he's out here playing with the big boys now. He talks big and he's got all his new hockey shit on, he's got to learn to play with the big boys," said Weezer.

Mike just glared at Weezer as the remainder of the players gathered around them. Weezer looked about and saw what was happening. The social pecking order of the neighborhood was based on who could 'take' who, with 'take' being a euphemism for kicking another's ass. Weezer outranked Mike. Whether Mike intended to challenge Weezer's standing with the group was irrelevant at this point. Weezer had to see it head on and deal with it.

"You wanna go?" Weezer said as he dropped his gloves to the ice.

"No," said Mike, looking down as he shuffled his brand-new skates. Mike knew his stature in the pecking order amid the neighborhood pugilists and wanted no part of Weezer, who was a notch or two above his grade, but to save a bit of face, he added "But just take it easy on the kid, alright?"

Weezer, satisfied that he had met and won the challenge, acknowledged Mike's honorable way out and nodded. He just did not feel like fighting. Especially over something stupid. Mike knew that Kevin deserved what he had gotten and was just doing the big brother bit, which Weezer appreciated. Plus, Mike was his best friend. He would have felt bad if he kicked Mike's ass. It would have ruined his day.

A disheveled Kevin skated up to Mike, still caked with snow and defiantly responded to Weezer.

"Weezer I can take whatever you got. Fuckhead."

"Shut up Kevin. Come on let's play," said Mike as he skated to center-ice.

The game continued and Kevin was no less annoying. Weezer did what he could to damper Kevin's fire. Whether it was an extra bit of muscle on a hip check or a surreptitious elbow in a scrum, Kevin would just ignore it and skate on, much to Weezer's frustration.

Finally, after switching the goalies' numerous times, the game came down to the next goal wins. The score was forgotten by everyone about an hour earlier. The older players were now showing up and would eventually take over the rink for another pickup game with far more skillful players.

Mike took the puck out from his zone and was quickly met by Weezer, who pestered him enough for Mike to pass the puck up-ice to Kevin. Kevin immediately shot the puck on Gibbons who blocked it, but the rebound came back out to Kevin and he quickly pushed it by an out of place Gibbons for the winning goal. Kevin immediately turned to Weezer with a winning grin and said, "How's that, you big fucking loser!"

Kevin continued to skate about the ice yelling out.

"Weezer you suck! You lose, you weezing son of a bitch! Suck it!"

Finally, Kevin skated up to Weezer and boldly said, "What you got now, Weezer?"

Weezer looked down at Kevin and calmly said, "There's no such thing as Santa Claus."

The grin and defiance quickly disappeared from Kevin's face.
"What?"

"You heard me you little fuck. Santa ain't real. He's bullshit."

Kevin burst into tears, turned, and made an angry beeline to the bench.

Mike skated up to Weezer.

"Jeez, what did you say to him?"

"The hard cool truth."

# CHAPTER 2

# THE EVENING AFTER CHRISTMAS 1969

The skating area was dark and empty as the last of the weary hockey players changed into their shoes. Bullethead was still waving his stick under a parked vehicle on 69th Street looking for his puck.

"You gonna be there all night?" yelled Mike from the bench next to the VFW hall.

"It's my brother's puck. He'll kill me if I lose it," was Bullethead's muffled response.

"Well, we ain't waitin' around. It's getting cold," yelled Weezer.

"Yeah, yeah. Go on you pussies. See you tomorrow. Aha! Got it!"

"Great. See you tomorrow. I'll sleep better knowing that you got your puck," said Weezer as he and Mike started the three block walk home.

"I thought that bus was going to stop," said Mike.

Weezer laughed and replied. "Yeah, it was a good thing that it just hit metal. If that puck hits a window, I'm sure it would have broke. It sure was loud, though."

After a pause, Weezer turned to Mike, "Think you'll get in trouble for Kevin?"

"For what? I didn't do anything. You're the one who told him the hard cool truth. Not me."

"But what about him walking home alone?"

"It's alright. It was still light out. I shouldn't catch too much flak."

The rapidly falling darkness helped to accentuate the overhead streetlights on Honore Street as the two boys walked along the shoveled sidewalk. Their visible, wispy breath trailed them like steam from a locomotive pulling the Polar Express. The foot-high piles of snow that lay parallel to the sidewalk on the front lawns, reflected the illumination from the streetlights and created a scene that would look beautiful on a Christmas card, but for the group in the middle of the block throwing frozen pieces of dog shit at a house across the street.

Father Cummins drove by in his 1969 Ford Fairlane, beeped his horn and waved to Weezer and Mike, who returned his wave. As he drove down Honore, he noticed a group gathered mid-block who were throwing frozen dog shit at a house across the street. He slowed to see who was in the crowd. He recognized Henry Teller among a group of high school kids. He stopped the car and rolled down the passenger side window. Most of the group approached the car.

"Good evening, guys," said Father Cummins.

"Evening Father," was the disjointed response.

"Merry Christmas to you all."

"Merry Christmas Father," came a more united answer.

"So, what are you guys up to?"

"Oh, nothing Father. Just shootin' the shit. Er, sorry Father," said Teller, the self-appointed spokesman for the group.

"This wouldn't be a welcoming party for the new neighbors, would it?"

"I'm not sure what you mean, Father. What new neighbors would you be talking about?" said Teller.

"C'mon Teller. The house with the squad car parked in front. Don't be a wise guy."

Teller looked over the top of Father Cummins' car at the idling Chicago Police car that sat immediately in front of the new neighbor's home. Its interior overhead light was on and was occupied by a lone police officer who seemed oblivious to anything that was not contained in the Chicago Sun-Times that he had spread out between himself and the steering wheel.

"Would you look at that. So that's where the new black family moved in. I didn't know Father, honest," said Teller.

"Teller don't be an asshole," said Father Cummins. He paused and gathered his composure. "I'd like to see you at Mass this Sunday. This is not the way, and you know it," he said.

"I'll be there, Father. You can count on that," replied Teller.

The peeved priest drove away while the group returned to their previous position, directly across the street from the idling police car.

"Not the way. Fuck him! It's easy for him to say that shit when he doesn't have to worry about a roof over his head. I've been here for over forty years. Raised four boys and buried a wife here. I ain't movin' nowhere," Teller said to anyone who would listen. He received a muted agreement from the remainder of the group as they settled in.

Teller took a plastic bag from his coat pocket and started to pass out frozen pieces of dog shit of various sizes to anyone who would take them. Once accepted, it was thrown at the house across the street where a small explosion of canine fecal shrapnel spread all about. Some of the pieces would bounce harmlessly off the siding of the house, some would carom off a window, while others would create a loud 'BANG' if they hit the aluminum front storm door, which eventually became the bullseye.  Small dents were now appearing on the bottom door panel and the concrete stoop looked as if someone had tossed a box of Raisenettes around like one would throw salt on an icy winter sidewalk.

Weezer and Mike approached the group.  Weezer recognized some of the older neighborhood guys, and asked, "Hey, what's going on?"

Eddie Jackson, a teenager with a bad haircut, bad acne, and a bad outlook, answered him.

"The niggers moved in across the street."

"So, you throw frozen dog shit at their house?  What's that do?" said Weezer in a genuinely confused manner.

"Sends them a message that we don't want them here," said Eddie as he flung a frozen turd at the house.

Teller approached the newcomers with an offer.

"Do you guys want some dog shit?"

The confused look on the boy's faces told Teller that he had to explain.

"Don't worry.  I got 'em from my own back yard.  I let them sit out there until they're good and frozen.  Don't have to worry about getting any on your hands and it makes them easier to throw.  Just take 'em and throw 'em.  Here."

Teller reached into his bag, pulled out a couple of frozen turds, took Mike's gloved hand and placed them in his palm before Mike even realized what he was accepting.

"God it's cold." said Weezer as he jumped in place.  He put his gear down on the sidewalk and turned to Mike and held out his gloved hand, "Gimmie one, will ya?"

Mike obliged and put a turd into Weezer's hand.  Weezer tossed it in the air like he was getting ready to throw out the first pitch at Sox Park and when it landed back into his gloved palm, he reared back in one motion and threw the clump at the house.  The throw was off target and split into a hundred pieces as it hit the side of the house.

"Damn. Gimmie another one."

Mike dutifully handed another piece to Weezer. This time he wound up and threw the cold hard brown projectile towards the door and, BAM! It made a noisy direct hit on the bottom of the door.

"Yeah, baby. Gimmie another."

Mike handed another, smaller, piece to Weezer.

"Last one," said Mike.

"That's alright. I'm getting cold."

"You guys running out? I've got plenty. I have five dogs, you know," said Teller.

"Yeah, we know," said Mike.

"Well, I've been out here since they moved in, last week. Before you know it, the whole block will be gone, and what am I supposed to do? My boys all work for the city so I can't just get up and move. Here's some more shit. Take all you want."

"Why don't you throw anything? You seem to have the most to lose. How come you're just giving this stuff away?" asked Weezer.

"I tried, but I can't make it across the street. My arm isn't what it once was."

"You want us to do your dirty work for you because you have a puss arm? Is that what this is?"

"No, no. You got it all wrong," pleaded Teller.

"Well, then. I'll throw another one, but you have to throw one first," said Weezer.

"I can't, I tell ya. It would be a waste of shit."

"Come on Mike," said Weezer. "Let's go."

"Wait. Okay, okay. I'll give it a shot," a deflated Teller said.

He walked to the curb from where they were standing on the sidewalk and turned around.

"I got to do it from here. I'm older than you."

Weezer nodded his approval and Teller turned back to face his target. He reached into his bag and pulled out a turd and paused. He knew he could not make the throw but, with a little luck he felt he could make it at least to the sidewalk and save face.

Or, if he was not lucky, his throw would land on top of the Chicago Police blue and white squad car that was parked in front of the house ostensibly to protect the inhabitants from any shenanigans that the neighbors may pull on them. Like what was currently happening.

Teller's throw landed on top of the squad car, shattering to pieces, the bulk of which rolled down the front windshield. An extremely angry police officer bolted out of the car and stormed up to the group on the sidewalk.

"Alright, that's enough of this crap! Who threw it?" he loudly demanded.

The group looked down at their feet and shuffled a bit, not wishing to rat on Teller, who was still standing at the curb. The officer turned and noticed the old man standing by himself with a bag of frozen dog shit and a guilty hangdog look on his face.

"Did you throw it?" the officer asked.

A visibly shaken Teller tried to get an answer out.

"Well, I ..."

"I told you to stay away from here! Didn't I? Didn't I? Okay, that's it for you. Dad go home! Right now. Just go home!"

The police officer turned to the rest of the group.

"The rest of you go home too. Now!"

Weezer and Mike picked up their gear, slung it over their shoulder as the rest of the group disbanded in various directions and walked down Honore with Teller for the half block to his home.

"So, Mr. Teller, what do you do with the left-over dog shit?" asked Mike.

"Oh, just freeze it.  Use it tomorrow.  There'll be a different cop."

After a silent walk for the remainder of the block, Teller went into his house and Weezer and Mike continued their journey home.

"That was kind of stupid," said Weezer.

"The dog shit?  Ha, I'm not worried.  Like he said, it was frozen, so I didn't get any on my gloves or hand."

"What?  No.  I'm talking about throwing the shit at the house.  What the hell was that?  It just didn't feel cool, you know.  It didn't feel right."

"Does everything have to feel right?  The blisters on my feet don't feel right, but down the road they'll be okay, and I'll be skating around in my new CCMs," said Mike casually.

Weezer was surprised at the simple logic of Mike's response.  He was not accustomed to Mike dispensing wisdom.

"That's pretty deep, man."

They silently continued their walk in what was now full night.

"God, my feet hurt," said Mike.

# CHAPTER 3

# DOWNTOWN
## Spring 1958

Tommy Mallon just turned eighteen and wanted a new life. He was neither a rebel nor a willing complier. He was neither left nor right, light nor dark, big nor small. He was comfortable in the middle. A reasonable person looks at things from the center of the issue. He liked to think that deductive reasoning and human logic should be applied to any decision one makes, at least the important ones, and just let it be at that. Maybe that was it. He deemed his decision to throw a pie out a seventh-floor window of Marshall Field's during a busy midweek afternoon as not important. Just a slight temporary deviance from his normal middle course of social etiquette.

He had an engagement ring in his pocket as he arrived to work that day and a firm resolution that it was to be his last day working as a busboy at Marshall Field's on State Street. His plan to flee his familial past and venture out on his own in some virtuous capacity was in full operational mode. He was to meet his beloved Claire Quinlan at the Berghoff, where they would resolve any issues they may have in a loving way, and he would open the velvet box and bare the ring to her astonished face.  At least that was his plan.

He had made his decision about three months earlier when he took the job at Field's.  His best friend Freddy Gallagher was working there and recommended Tommy for the job.  Freddy needed the job at Field's to supplement his income from what he considered his real career pursuit, a life of crime.

Today, however, was a big day for both Tommy and Freddy. Tommy was finally leaving his Uncle Wally's sphere of influence and voyaging out into the world.  The real world of paychecks, and an occupation rather than underworld specialties.  For Freddy, he had been the apprentice behind Tommy for the past four years, smiling while holding in his distain, doing the shit jobs without verbal complaint and now he would move up and have the title of Wally's Number One along with the boost in income.  His cut with Wally would increase and as such, he did not need the Field's job anymore. In fact, he hated the job so much that he recruited Tommy to make their last day a memorable one.

Tommy and Freddy would throw the pies out of the window and run like hell.  They figured that it would take a couple of seconds of free-falling from the seventh floor until the pies would either splatter on the Randolph Street sidewalk or hit some poor innocent bastard who happened to be in the wrong place at the wrong time.  A couple more seconds would pass to allow anyone who saw the pies splatter to pinpoint where they came from.  And a couple of minutes to relay this information to the proper authorities, i.e., their bosses, which all together would certainly be enough time to get away and get back to where they should have been in the first place.

Tommy thought that the pies were apple.  He smelled the apple-cinnamon scent that emanated from the symmetrical slits that were cut into the top of each pie.  Tommy and Freddy had pilfered the tasty projectiles from the dessert cart that was standing by itself in the kitchen of the Bowl & Basket restaurant, one of eight restaurants that occupied the seventh floor of Marshal Field's Department Store.

They looked about to make sure that no one saw them as they took their pies and shenanigans into the utility room. Acting like the immature morons that they were, they attempted to stifle their laughter by holding their noses, which just defeated the purpose, and they ended up making unnatural loud snorting noises.

The utility room was a large closet with a small window that swung open, to vent any weird aromas or fumes from cleaning liquids that were dumped into the big industrial sink just below it.

Quickly, they closed the door behind them and took a last desperate look at each other, as they realized that they were now at the point of no return.  Their laughing ceased.

"Are you ready?" Tommy asked.

"Yeah, let's do this," Freddy quickly replied.

Freddy reached over the old sink and swung the window open. Instantly the vibrant hum from one of the busiest shopping districts in the world filled the air.

"On three," Tommy said.  Freddy nodded as he went into a shot-putter's stance with his pie almost resting on his right shoulder.

"One."

Freddy focused intently on his task.

"Two."

Suddenly Tommy felt a rush of something.  Was it fear?  The pie started to quiver in his loaded right hand.  Was he sure he wanted to do this?  It had been a good ride working for Fields, why mess it up now?  If he got caught, it would follow him around for the rest of his life.

"Gee Mr. Mallon, we would have loved to give you this 100k job, but there's this pie thing.  Can you explain that?"

"Two and a half," he blurted.

Freddy's pie was launched out the window.

"Three!"

Tommy's pie followed.

"You fucker!" Freddy hollered in a snickered whisper as they scrambled to leave the scene of the crime. With the two of them desperately trying to get out of the small utility room at the same time, it became a Stooge-like episode. Finally, Tommy backed up to allow space for the door to open and Freddy shot out first. They went their separate ways from there, Freddy to the English Room and Tommy back to the Walnut Room. If anyone has any questions later, he was at his dining room bus station the whole time.

With the dastardly last-day-on-the-job prank completed, it became a nervous afternoon for Tommy. He went about his business filling the water glasses of the lunchtime guests and clearing dirty dishes.

The patrons of the Walnut Room in the Marshal Field's flagship store were generally an older and more genteel crowd. In this room the ladies still wore hats and gloves when they sipped their tea. Lunch at the Walnut Room had become a tradition for a lot of the regular guests and the day was filled with properly dressed matrons patiently standing behind the velvet ropes that guarded the entrance to the room. It wasn't the type of place for a power lunch or a quick bite. Not only was the food savored here, but the entire atmosphere had become a bit of an old-school dining experience. The dark wood paneled walls with brass fixtures and a high ceiling with chandeliers gave it a turn-of-the-century feeling, like you had just spent the day at the Columbian Exposition and now enjoyed supper before going home.

Finally, Tommy's shift was over and after a silent sigh of relief that he was not being led out in handcuffs, he walked out of the kitchen and to the employee locker room, where everyone milled about as they changed from the greasy white bus outfits into their street clothes.  Tommy said "good-bye" and "keep in touch" with everyone.  He and Freddy walked into the rest of their lives, wherever that may be.

They exited on to State Street and encountered a breezy spring afternoon as they walked south on the busy sidewalk.

"You meeting Wally?" asked Tommy.

"Yeah.  Out at Sportsman's.  He's gotta tip.  Want in?" replied Freddy.

"No, no.  I'm done with that shit.  Going to meet Claire."

"Where?"

"The Berghoff.  Hopefully they'll serve me.  I forgot my ID."

"The Berghoff huh?  Are you gonna pop the question?"

"I'm planning on it," said Tommy as he pulled out the dark blue velvet box from his jacket pocket and showed it to Freddy.

"Serious shit.  Ok.  Are you sure she's gonna show up?"

"What do you mean?"

"Well, she did say you guys were through after you broke her brother's finger the other night. You heard that, right?"

"Well, yeah, but you know how she is.  She'll forget about it and move on."

"Not while she's looking at the cast on Chet's hand every day. You really got him good."

"Well, he shouldn't talk shit about Wally.  You make a bet, you pay.  There's no gray area there.  I just kind of lost it, I guess. Shouldn't have done it. But I'm not collecting anymore.  She'll get over it.  So will he."

"Okay," said Freddy.  "But whether she shows or not, you're not getting this gig back from Wally.  It's mine, Jack.  If you do come back, it'll be under me.  Capisce?"

"Not going to be an issue.  Trust me."

Freddy pulled out a cigarette, lit it, took a drag, and displayed a flash of seriousness that sent a twinge of concern through Tommy, but he swatted it away.

"I'm gonna treat myself tonight and cab it to the track. It's good to be making some dough for once," said Freddy as he approached the curb and hailed a bright yellow taxi.

Tommy watched the cab drive off then continued west on Adams to the Berghoff, an old-time, wood paneled, brass railed restaurant and bar that featured the world's greatest soft pretzels that just begged for a splash of mustard.

As he gave his eyes time to acclimate to the dimly lit bar area, he looked about and sensed that the crowded establishment may work to his advantage. A hurried bartender was far less likely to ask for an ID. The bartenders, wrapped in aprons and clad in white shirts with black bow ties and vests, were busy serving the late lunch crowd, washing glasses, wiping the bar and keeping tabs on the money. Confident that unless you looked like you were twelve the bartender would not card you, Tommy motioned for the bartender in a busy corner of the bar and ordered a beer.

"Got an ID?" said the bartender.

Tommy reacted by reaching back for his wallet, a futile gesture that would only prolong the embarrassment, but the harried bartender put a stein of gold lager in front of him and waited patiently to be paid. Tommy realized that the busy bartender had forgotten about his ID request or blown it off and he immediately produced a five-dollar bill, handed it to the bartender who left and returned with four-dollars and a quarter and placed it on the bar. Tommy grinned like someone who pulled something off, grabbed the four singles from the bar and made his way to a standing table in the window, near the door, from where he could watch for Claire's arrival. He looked at his watch. It was a little before three.

Tommy tasted his beer and thought about Freddy's words. In a worst-case scenario, if this didn't work out, he could always rely on his Uncle Wally. He remembered when he was young, Uncle Wally would always have something in hand when he would arrive at the apartment to pick up Dad for their evening shenanigans. It could be a comic book, a candy bar or even a pack of baseball cards, it didn't really matter. Tommy liked the anticipation more than the actual gift. When he would see Uncle Wally at the door, he knew he was in for something good. He also remembered that sometimes when he was up or awoken by Dad and Wally getting home, his mother's moods would vary when the two revelers would arrive. Sometimes Dad would bring home a brand-new dress, other times he would bring home a sad story about how some "nag" caused his dream bets to fail or that Uncle Wally took too many cards in a game of poker. The sad stories far outnumbered the dresses if Tommy remembered right.

Wally was a slightly rotund man, who could have been an extra on any movie set that involved a pie fight. He lacked any facial hair except for his trademark hairy mole that protruded just above his left eyebrow. His black hairline was slowly retreating from the top of his forehead, so he wore a grey fedora most of the time, tilted to the right, just as Robert Mitchum wore his. Wally had seen a picture of Mitchum in one of those Hollywood fan magazines and liked the look and aura that Mitchum gave off.

"Robert Mitchum is a man's man," he said to Tommy one day after exiting the bathroom with the magazine in hand that had the Mitchum picture in it. Tommy felt that Wally had more in common with Oliver Hardy than Robert Mitchum, but never told him that. Despite his big fish-small pond position in the neighborhood, Wally was insecure about certain physical aspects of himself. Later, when Tommy was older, he heard a tipsy and remorseful Wally wonder aloud as to why he always had to pay for sex. Tommy had no answer. Tommy was aware of Wally's insecurities, and he would rather pull his own eyes out than hurt Wally's feelings in any way. That's why it was so difficult to tell him that he would be finding another line of work.

Wally anticipated and accepted Tommy's decision and never showed his disappointment. He did have Freddy Gallagher to replace him, but any reaction was tempered by the fact that Wally also was aware that Tommy had made a promise to his departed mother that he would join the priesthood. The fact that Tommy left for a woman rather than religion did not bother him as both were deep mysteries to him. As far as Wally was concerned, Tommy just traded one bag of cats for another.

Tommy looked at his watch. It was almost three-fifteen. He took a sip of beer.

Tommy Mallon grew-up in St. Justin Martyr parish near 69th and Ashland. The only son of Catherine, a Catholic widow. When Tommy was ten, his father, Richard, passed away from mysterious causes. Thereafter, young Tommy's mission in life, per Catherine, was to follow all her mandates and wishes. Catherine instilled in him that this was his spiritual duty in life, to appease and ensure that Catherine's life would be eased as needed because Catherine was the victim of Richard's circumstances. Richard was now in the afterlife (wherever that may be), and could not be hurt anymore, but Catherine remained in the current life and was left to endure more of the trials that lay before her before she reached the afterlife (surely Heaven). Tommy dutifully accepted his new responsibility and purpose.

Catherine had her own private interpretation of the Catholic faith. For example, she rarely went to mass, but always went to confession. Tommy wondered what sins she could possibly be atoning for. It confounded him that she would be with any sin at all, as she had no bad habits and acted like an eccentric angel while in front of him.  Then one day the pilot light in the stove went out.  She lit a match to light the burner and once it lit, the burner flame flared up and singed some hairs on her arm.

"Oh shit!" she exclaimed.  Suddenly it dawned on Tommy that the reason she went to confession every week was that she had a potty mouth.  It was the first and last time that he had heard her swear, but it provided a suitable explanation for Tommy at the time, and he let it be at that.

Tommy glanced again at his watch.  He continued to nurse his beer as he remembered Catherine as a sort of unwilling passenger in a car that was on a long trip. Not a kidnap victim, but someone who was on a mission that had to get accomplished.  A joyless excursion of necessity.

He remembered her black, straight hair that was held in place in the back of her head with a comb that allowed the hair to flow down her back almost to her thin delicate waste.  Like Tommy, she was neither short nor tall.  She was neither beautiful nor ugly.  She had normal features and clear white, almost pale, skin that sagged over the lonely years after Richard passed away.  But she did not exist in the middle, as Tommy now did.  She was extreme in her beliefs, no matter how unconventional they were.  Eventually she turned humorless and withdrawn, which may have influenced how he remembered her physical features.  He felt she had become numb to joy.  When she commanded him to consider the priesthood, he immediately promised that he would.  He wanted to give her something that would make the car ride worthwhile.

He was gazing out of the front window of the bar and watched as a couple entered, scanned the crowded bar, and opted for the empty table next to Tommy.  As they took their jackets off, the man nodded to Tommy.  The man hung the jackets on a standing coat rack in the corner of the bar.  He went to the bar and returned with a beer for him and some sort of bronze colored mixed drink for her. It had a cherry in it.

Tommy could not help but overhear their conversation as they were close and loud. They had just caught a matinee of a new Hitchcock movie, *Vertigo,* and were raving about the actors in the film, Jimmy Stewart and Kim Novak, who, according to the woman, grew up in the Chicago area. Tommy was not aware of that. He was also not aware of who Kim Novak was, but he was aware of Jimmy Stewart.

When Tommy was twelve years old and Richard had been dead for a couple of years, Catherine took Tommy to the Highland Theater to see *The Greatest Show on Earth*, a film about the shenanigans that occur behind the scenes of a circus tour. Jimmy Stewart played a clown who never took his makeup off. It was not until weeks later that Tommy saw what Jimmy Stewart looked like and became a fan. It was a beautiful film, shot in Technicolor, with amazing high-wire acts, trapeze artists and elephants.

The Highland Theater was on 79th and Ashland, so Catherine and Tommy caught the three o'clock show. After the movie ended, they exited the theater to find heavy rain outside. Unprepared, Catherine held her purse over her head while crossing 79th Street with Tommy in tow to catch the oncoming bus heading back north on Ashland. The pelting rain made it hard for Tommy to see as he held Catherine's hand while crossing the busy street. He did not see the large truck knock Catherine twenty feet in the air. She landed on the pavement with a lifeless thud.

He had felt her hand leave his and then he stopped in the middle of the intersection, blind and wet. He heard some commotion and distant voices. Despite the rain he could see the contorted body of Catherine lying face down on the wet pavement. A small stream of blood wound its way from the side of her head down the sloping asphalt, flowing into the sewer grate.

His next memory was standing next to Catherine's still open grave at the cemetery gazing at the casket while shaking his head. Father Callaghan came up from behind him and said, "It's God's will son. Let it be at that."

For some reason, he did not feel bad about breaking his priest-hood promise to his mother. The joyous feeling of falling in love was tempered by the fact that he felt bad about not feeling bad.  But he had fallen for Claire and was about to follow through on his plan to ask her to marry him and the bad feeling would eventually fade away.  At least that was what he was telling himself.

Claire Quinlan was a neighborhood girl.  She had caught his attention about eight months earlier when he was accompanying Uncle Wally on one of his collection runs.  Wally saw Claire and her brother, Chet, in Dan's Hamburgers on 71st Street.  Wally did a serious U-turn and pulled into Dan's parking lot.  He jumped out of the car and dragged Chet by his shirt-collar from the hamburger stand.

"Chet, I've been very patient.  Very patient," said Wally in a matter-of-fact tone.

"I know, I know," Chet responded.  "For sure this Friday.  I promise Wally.  I promise."

Wally released Chet and straightened out the front of his shirt.

"Chet, you are such a lucky motherfucker.  You're lucky I'm such a sweetheart and we are in a public place."  Wally turned away as if he was going back to his car but stopped and turned back to Chet.

"Aw, fuck it," he said and grabbed Chet by the shirt again.

Just then Claire walked out of Dan's.  Still in the car, Tommy watched the seventeen-year-old girl licking a vanilla ice cream cone. He got out of the car.  She looked at him.  He looked at her.  It was over.

Wally continued to threaten Chet with the loss of various appendages of his body while pulling him around the parking lot by his shirt and slapping him in the back of the head.  Chet cowered and made promises.  During this collection procedure, Claire and Tommy's eyes never left each other's gaze.

* * * * * * * *

It was now almost four o'clock and Tommy finished his beer.  He looked about the now less crowded bar area and realized that any effort to procure a second beer would be for naught.  Even so, he approached the bar and ordered a soft pretzel from the bartender.

"Anything else?" the bartender asked.

Tommy decided to push his luck.

"Yeah, give me a lager."

"Got an ID?" asked the bartender.

"I'll just take the pretzel," Tommy responded as he put a dollar on the bar and walked back to his table with his pretzel and pride in hand.

He took a bite from the pretzel.  It would have to last him until Claire arrived.  In his haste and embarrassment, he neglected to get any mustard from the bar, so the pretzel was a bit dry and was turning into what was basically a ball of dough.  Fine, thought Tommy, the longer I chew, the longer I can occupy this convenient spot in the window of the bar.

Tommy gazed out the window.  The afternoon shadows were growing longer as were the odds of Claire appearing through the front door.  The slow realization that Claire would not show was now seeping into Tommy's mind.

Maybe he was a little too rough with Chet.  In hindsight, he grudgingly conceded to himself that he probably should not have broken Chet's pinky last week.  At least not with Claire present.  Chet had let him in their house for a collection visit but unfortunately, Chet had been drinking and chose to be belligerent about the money he owed Wally.  Tommy was not aware that Claire was home.  He recalled the scream from Claire at the high-pitched crack of Chet's pinky bone as she walked into the room just as he was doing the heinous act.

The scream bothered him more than that crack.  He took another bite from the pretzel and chewed as he continued to look out the window.

Realizing that he was approaching the socially acceptable time limit to nurse a soft pretzel, Tommy put the last of it into his mouth and left the bar.  It was a bit chillier than it was two hours before when he walked in.  A light rain was starting, so he stopped to button his jacket.

Adams Street was crowded with the rush hour crowd, marching to their bus stops or train stations, most with their heads down and hands in their pockets.  Tommy looked about for an inconspicuous area where he could spit out the wad of pretzel, but the sidewalk was far too crowded to chance it.

He reached into his pocket and pulled out the blue velvet box and opened it.  He looked at the ring and slowly tilted the box back and forth so the neon light from the bar sign would reflect in the prism of the full karat rock.  The colors entranced him.  He pulled the ring from the box and put it in his pants pocket.  He then spit the wad of pretzel into the box, closed it and deposited it in a waste basket at the end of the block.

He continued walking east to State Street and then turned south.

 The rain on the street reflected the now awakening myriad of lights, from the basic white streetlights above to the neon signs that flashed BILLIARDS, BURLESQUE, LOANS.  Tommy had crossed under the Van Buren El tracks out of the Loop and into the less respectable area where less respectable businesses flourished.

He reached into his pocket and pulled out the ring.  He clenched it in his right hand and put both hands in his jacket pockets.  The rain was now dripping from his hatless head and starting to roll down his back in slow cold beads. He raised his collar and dug his chin into his chest and kept walking.

Tommy did not notice the men with three-day old beards and short cigarettes hanging from their lips huddled under the awnings and in the doorways of the seedy establishments that lined South State Street. Heavy thoughts bounced about in Tommy's head as he walked the gauntlet of the needy. He suddenly stopped and looked up at the large and colorful fully lit three-story sign that hung above the front door of the Pacific Garden Mission.

The horizontal part of the sign read "CHRIST DIED FOR OUR SINS." Beneath it was a large cross with the word JESUS on the horizontal part and the word SAVES extending down from the S in JESUS.

Very clever, thought Tommy. He took his right hand from his pocket, opened it and looked at the ring. He walked into a storefront beneath a large electric sign that said PAWN.

# CHAPTER 4

# SPORTSMAN'S PARK
# Spring 1958

Wally was sitting by himself in the covered grandstands at Sportsman's Park, at the finish line. He was studying the racing program, checking off here, underlining there and making insightful notations on the margins of the page. He looked like a scholar at work. His fedora tilted up on his head and a pair of reading glasses hung precariously at the end of his nose.

His focus was interrupted by Freddy Gallagher. "Hey," said a smiling Freddy as he took a seat next to Wally.

Wally turned from his racing program to the unwanted intruder who dared to break his attention to the day's harness racing program. He looked at his watch and turned back to Freddy and said, "You're late."

Freddy's grin quickly dissolved as he started his explanation.

"I had to stop by the Ridge Tap. I knew Bixby would be there, he owes..."

Wally cut him off.

"I don't fucking care. These races do not wait for nobody. Including you, you stupid fuck. Get these down to the paddock now." He put a small folded, piece of paper into Freddy's hand.

"But first, you take this to the top of the grandstand, open it, memorize the numbers and races on it and then tear it up into tiny bits and swallow it. All of it."

Freddy's eyes gave away his confusion as to whether Wally meant to eat the paper literally.

"You eat every scrap of it and swallow it."

The look of confusion vanished from Freddy's face and was replaced with dread.

"Then you haul your little ass down to the paddock and ask for Lucky. He's expecting you. You give him the numbers on this paper that you are going to shit out later and tell him that we probably won't be back tonight. You got that, Einstein?"

Freddy nodded in silence.

"Now go. I'll be watching every step."

Freddy turned and walked up the aisle of the grandstand to the enclosed seating area at the top. He looked down at Wally, about twenty rows away. Wally was watching him open the paper.

It simply said, 6 in 7. Freddy repeated the sequence slowly to himself.

"Six in seven."

"Six in seven."

He repeated it to himself at a faster rate.

"Six in seven. Six in seven. Six in seven."

He paused and looked back down at Wally.

"Got it."

Freddy tore the paper into tiny bits and stuffed the entire wad into his mouth. It was a mistake.

Freddy realized that you cannot chew paper like you do food. Most food can easily be processed by simple up and down chewing.

The chewing breaks the food down to smaller pieces to allow you to cleanly swallow without clogging your throat.

Paper isn't like that. Paper needed a more orbital chewing, not really chewing but a rending of the paper by a sideways motion, mostly by the molars. Chewing the paper like it was food only compressed it into a hard mass that makes it extremely difficult to swallow, if not downright impossible.

This all clearly came to Freddy in an instant while he struggled to breathe with a large wad of compressed paper in his throat.

He wildly flayed his arms trying to attract somebody's attention, but the only people who saw him were Wally, who was too far to offer any assistance and two sotted horseplayers watching from behind the glass partition that divided the indoor seating area from the grandstand.

"I want what he's having," said one of the horseplayers to the other.

Desperately trying to breathe, Freddy grabbed his throat while the shade of his face started to turn an eerie blue.

Suddenly a pair of arms wrapped around Freddy's torso and lurched upward on his chest in hard rhythmic actions. Freddy felt the paper move up in his throat and managed a quick grasp of air before it seemed to fall back and block his airway again. The arms unwrapped from Freddy's body, bent him over at the waist, and banged on the upper portion of his back. The wad of paper finally ejected from his throat. Freddy stood upright and loudly took in a huge rush of air. He then bent over again and put his hands on his knees, taking in more air but in a slower and quieter manner.

He turned to look at his savior and saw a smiling Tommy Mallon.

"You alright, man?" asked Tommy.

Freddy stood erect and faced Tommy.

"Yeah, yeah. Thanks man."

Freddy turned and looked at Wally, still in his seat twenty rows down. Wally pointed at his watch and visibly scolded Freddy with his dark furrowed eyebrows and a scowl that scared the hell out of Freddy. He turned back to Tommy.

"Hey, gotta go."

Freddy raced down the grandstand aisle and disappeared into the ground level crowd.

Tommy walked down and sat near Wally, leaving a seat between them.

"What was that all about? You had him eating paper?"

"Trying to train your successor. He can be as dumb as a box of rocks sometimes. But I'll make it work. What are you doing here?"

"She didn't show," Tommy sadly said as he turned his gaze out over the illuminated track.

"I'm sorry to hear that," said Wally. He also turned his visual attention to the track as the sulkies for the first race were approaching the mobile starting gate that was attached to the rear of a glossy black 1958 Chevy Bel Air convertible.

"Take a look at that Chevy Bel Air now while it's clean. Light rain falling, gonna get sloppy," Wally said while still looking out over the track. He turned back to Tommy.

"So now what?"

"I want back in," said Tommy without hesitation.

"You sure about that? You've always wanted to do the right thing."

"Screw women and religion. They are what's wrong with the world."

Wally paused and rubbed his cheek.

"Look, Tommy, I'm not going to disagree with you. You're right. But do you think a life of crime contributes anything positive to the world?"

"It worked out okay for Robin Hood."

"Robin Hood? So, you wanna rob from the rich and give to the poor? Is that it?"

"Well, after my cut, yeah, sure."

Wally shook his bewildered head as Freddy appeared at the end of the row.

"Done, just like you said," he reported as he sat next to Tommy.

Just then the starting bell rang. The temporarily clean Chevy Bel Air began to move, with the horses pulling the big-wheeled sulkies, building momentum behind the car, each in their assigned gate. Eventually the car and the starting gate pulled away from the field of trotters and the race was on with the outside trotters collapsing as close to the rail as they could.

The trio watched the race with detached passion as no one had anything wagered. Wally had a personal credo that he would not bet on races that he did not know the outcome beforehand. It just made good business sense, he thought.

As the trotters ran on the far straight-away, Tommy took Wally's racing program to look at the field for the second race. He had a hundred and fifty dollars burning a hole in his pocket from the pawn shop for the ring he had bought for Claire. He was looking to turn it into a larger stash by the end of the night.

The trotters crossed the finish line. A horse named Biggie Wiggie won the race after going off at three to one odds.

Big deal thought Tommy as he continued to peruse the racing program. He was looking for a larger hit than three to one. He was looking for longshot all the way. He turned to Uncle Wally.

"What do you think about Rubber Ball in the second race?" he asked.

Wally turned to Tommy. "Who?"

Tommy held the program up to Wally and showed him Rubber Ball's numbers from his past races that were in the program.

"See. Pretty good times in the past three races. Does pretty well in the mud too."

"No. There's a reason I have a line crossed through his name. You're looking at the time numbers, which is all well and good but doesn't mean a damn thing. You gotta look here."

Wally pointed to the name of Rubber Ball, which was printed in bold letters and then trailed his finger to the sulky driver's name printed in less glaring letters just below the horse's name.

"See here. Schneider. He's a piece of shit that can be bought with a nickel bag. There's a reason he's going off at twenty to one. No one thinks he's gonna win. Simple as that."

"But the mud," countered Tommy. "How can you predict that?"

"Okay, do what you want."

"I've got a feeling. I'm going to bet on him."

Tommy rose from his seat to go place his bet, leaving Freddy and Wally to sit in silence while they watched the tractor groom the track between races. Finally, Freddy broke the silence.

"So, what's up with Tommy?"

"He's coming back," said a distracted Wally. "She stood him up."

Freddy stewed in silence. This was not what he had anticipated. In his mind, Tommy would sail off to marriageville or religionville and except for a Christmas card once a year, would never be heard from again, while Freddy reaped the benefits of being Wally's number one guy.

A distraught Freddy grabbed the program and paged through the races, trying to make heads or tails from Wally's markings. When he got to the seventh race, he noticed the six- horse circled two or three times and realized it was the race and horse that he had told Lucky about. Hmmm.

Tommy came back with his betting ticket for the long shot in the second race. Wally shook his head and said, mostly to himself, "You'll learn."

The second race went off. Rubber Ball finished far out of the money. A determined Tommy paged through the program again for the next race. The rain had let up and he used that as an explanation as to why Rubber Ball did not finish in the money.

"Track was too dry. Not a true mud track like he needed."

For the third race Tommy went with a fifteen to one nag, Heavenly Bliss, that barely crossed the finish line.

"That's alright," said Tommy. "I just need one for the night."

Tommy's betting luck did not get any better for the next four races. He found himself counting his remaining funds.

The seventh race arrived, and Wally turned to Tommy. "Okay, enough with the long shots. Bet the six-horse now. Put everything you have left on this horse to win. You too Freddy. Go. Now."

Tommy and Freddy went together to make their bets. After a few minutes, they came back, each with fifty-dollar bets on the six-horse, Pearls Before Swine.

The seventh race started off behind the now muddy Chevy Bel Air. In the first turn, Pearls Before Swine, at ten to one odds, took the lead and never relinquished it.

When the race was over, Freddy and Tommy jumped up and down like it was their first win at a horse race, which it was. Wally grinned at his two underlings. He handed Freddy a large stack of betting tickets, all showing ten-dollar bets on Pearls Before Swine.

"Now you guys take these up to various betting windows and bring me back the cash. Oh, and cash your own tickets."

When they returned, they gave Wally the money from his tickets, about five thousand dollars. He peeled off two fifties and gave them one each.

"That ought to help," said Wally. "I'm going now. You guys can stay if you like. I'm done for the evening."

"We'll stay," said Tommy. "There's only three races left."

"Okay," said Wally.  "See you at home.  Freddy, I want you to go down and see Lucky and tell him that's it for tonight and that I'll see him at the regular place."

"Got it," said Freddy.

Wally left, leaving behind his racing program that Freddy immediately grabbed.  He sat down and opened it, flipping through the pages, pretending that he knew what he was looking at.

"So, who do you like in the eighth?" Freddy casually asked Tommy.  "Oh, and I hear you're coming back?"

"Yeah, I guess so.  I'm sorry Freddy but she just left me hanging. I certainly don't feel too holy after that experience."

"So, you've given up on the whole priest thing?  Just like that?"

Tommy turned pensive.  He tried to gather the words to explain why he made his decision but couldn't.

"Ah, Freddy.  I wish this was an easy decision.  You'd think, right? Do I want to walk straight and maybe make a difference or become a criminal?  Remain a criminal."

"It's not always as simple as that. Look at me."

Tommy turned and looked at Freddy.  He started to laugh.

"Yeah, you're pretty simple."

"Fuck you.  Simple.  Huh.  What's this mean?"

Freddy held up the program and pointed to a set of numbers on the page for the eighth race.  Tommy looked at it.

"It tells you by how far the horse either won or lost the race. See, this says he finished second by two lengths, or furlongs.  So, you know it didn't get blown out in the last race."

"Oh.  I get it," said Freddy as he continued perusing the program.

"What I need is a sign," Tommy said.

"A sign?"

"Yeah, something to point me in the right direction, to make the right decision.  I'm not entirely sold on going back to working for my Uncle Wally."

"Hmm," said Freddy as he continued reading the program.  He turned the page to the tenth race where something caught his eye.  He stared at it for a minute as the gears of ingenuity revolved in his head.  Then something clicked.

"I gotta go down and see Lucky for Wally.  Be right back," Freddy said as he quickly headed down the main aisle.

Tommy opened the program to the ninth race as there was not enough time for him to place his bet for the eighth.  His eyes went to the trotter with the longest odds.  Ah, Ronny's Memory is going off at fifteen to one, and it was not crossed out by Uncle Wally like the other horses, so why not?  Tommy went to the window and placed another long shot bet.

It did not go well as Ronny's Memory barely finished sixth in a field of six.

Freddy returned after the ninth race.  The betting windows were now accepting bets on the tenth and final race as Tommy sat slumped in his seat.  His long-shot system was not working.  He was thinking of blowing off the tenth race and just leaving.

"You want to go now?" Tommy asked Freddy.  He looked up from the program and turned to Tommy.

"You want your sign?"

"What?"

"Your sign.  The sign you wanted to make your decision."

"Why?  What do you have?"

Freddy handed Tommy the racing program opened to the tenth race.

"Look at the number five horse."

Tommy looked at it and read out loud the horse's name.

"Apple of Momma's Eye."

"Now look at the board," said Freddy.

The current odds-on Apple of Momma's Eye were at fifteen to one.

"There's your fucking sign!  Right there.  What type of pies did we throw out of the window today?  Remember?"

"Apple.  Apple pie," Tommy softly muttered.

"Who'd you make your promise to?" Freddy continued.

Tommy paused to make the karma computations in his head.  A vision of his mother laying in the middle of 79th Street popped in his head.  He started to head to the betting window.  Freddy also got up, but Tommy put his hand on Freddy's shoulder.  He sat back down.

"No.  You can't bet on this race.  It's my sign.  I can't have you fucking it all up on me."

"Okay man.  I certainly wouldn't want to screw up your sign."

Tommy left for the betting window.  Freddy pulled a Marlboro and a book of matches from his jacket pocket, lit the cigarette, and exhaled the smoke upward in a steady stream of smiling self-congratulations.

Tommy returned from making his bet.

"Put the whole wad on her," said Tommy.  "Oh, and thanks for not betting.  I really appreciate it."

"No problem amigo."

Apple of Momma's Eye, the five horse, entered its starting gate behind the muddy Chevy Bel Air, along with the other seven horses in the race.  Apple of Momma's Eye did indeed end up as the long shot of the race and stayed at fifteen to one odds.

The starting bell went off and the muddy Chevy pulled away from the starting field with Apple of Momma's Eye in the middle of the mass of horseflesh and wheels, keeping pace with the group.  As the pack came out of the first turn, the congestion eased and the distances between the sulkies grew larger as some of the trotters were already starting to fade.  Apple of Momma's Eye remained with the leaders.

Out of the second turn, more trotters started to fade and as they arrived to start the home stretch, only three horses were in contention. Milly's Apron, the favorite, Dreamboat, and Apple of Momma's Eye. Dreamboat tried to come wide to pass the other two horses, but the technique failed, and Dreamboat faded. It was now Milly's Apron and Apple of Momma's Eye on the inside rail, side by side, racing for the finish line with Milly's Apron leading by a nose.

Tommy stood up and started yelling, "C'mon Momma! C'mon Momma!"

Milly's Apron had a three-foot lead as the horses entered the home stretch. Suddenly, the right wheel of the sulky that Milly's Apron was pulling came off from the axle and spun away, causing both the sulky and the driver to be thrown in the air. Milly's Apron came to an immediate stop, allowing Apple of Momma's Eye to blow past and cross the finish line to win the race.

Tommy erupted in elation and turned to Freddy.

"That was the sign! That was the sign!"

"Well, if that ain't a sign of something, I don't know what the fuck is," said Freddy.

That evening Freddy stood next to the dresser in his bedroom as he started to take his clothes off for bed. He and Tommy had shared a cab from the track. Tommy explained that he would not be working for Wally as the sign directed him to the light. He would be Father Tom Mallon. He felt bad about preventing Freddy from making a bet so in his newfound charitable light, he gave Freddy the six grand he won on the race.

Freddy pulled the cash from his right pocket and laid it on the dresser top. He reached into his left pocket and pulled out another six thousand dollars. This wad was from the bet he made on his way back from his second visit with Lucky that he did not tell Tommy about.

He reached back into his left pocket and pulled out a large axle-nut and washer. He looked at the pieces of dirty hardware and smiled. He put them in the top drawer, along with the wads of cash and then finished getting undressed and slipped beneath the blanket.

He reached up and turned off the light on his nightstand then slept like a baby.

# CHAPTER 5

# THE NAZI JOINT
## April 1970

It was a wet morning. The constant spring rains had saturated Murray Park's grassless infield to the point where it would take the entire day for the sun to dry out the thin layer of mud on the infield, if the sun came out at all. That is why Weezer and Mike found themselves in Billy Duffy's garage that morning. The main door was wide open while the rain outside slowed to an annoying trickle. They bickered with the other attendees, swapping and trading whatever the hot commodity was at that moment.

As had been for the past half year, automobile stickers were the rage. Among the most valuable were the iconic "STP" sticker, the Bardahl Man and a bad-ass Woody the Woodpecker type character who wore a mean scowl and had a cigar hanging out of his beak that somehow sold automobile mufflers. The stickers were the main commodity at that moment but there were certainly other items that were bartered. Classic items like comic books and baseball cards were present during any new fad and once there was even a group effort when they tried to collect different insects to make a bug zoo.

That lasted about three days until the zoo inhabitants started to die. They ended up feeding the survivors to a large spider that they had caught and affectionately named Herman. Herman lived like a king for about a week until they ran out of bugs and interest. Then they released him back to the wild where they had originally caught him, in the alley behind Bullethead's house next to a large telephone pole where some weeds grew through the large cracks in the concrete.

The swap meet was in full bloom when Bullethead walked in the garage holding something under his shirt. Weezer's first thought was his dad's Playboy magazine. Last fall, Bullethead snuck one of his dad's magazines to the garage and made out like a bandit ripping out pictures and swapping them for big returns. The pictures themselves fetched a nice price, but when he cleanly detached the centerfold from the staples, unfolded it and held it up for all to see, the bidding turned rabid and he walked away with ten STP stickers, four Bardahl Men and a Louie Aparicio card. The haul was enormous and is still spoken about in legendary terms.

But today he had something different. As his presence became known, each boy in the garage stopped whatever deal he was in the midst of and turned toward Bullethead, each anticipating that the item he had under his shirt would be up for bidding, picture by picture. Finally, as all eyes were on him, he slowly pulled out the items and fanned them like a poker hand. Instantly everyone recognized his wares, and a collective awe filled the garage, as this was something new that nobody had.

For the past couple of weeks, hand bills, flyers and stickers had been popping up in the neighborhood plastered on street signs and on the wall beneath viaducts, some with stereotypical depictions of country blacks coming to the big city with suitcase in hand looking to move to the neighborhood and that there was nothing to be done about the dark immigration than to support the American Nazi

Party. Others were less subtle and had a black swastika with skull and crossbones overlaid on it with the words, "Nigger Beware," scrawled beneath it. There were other pieces of literature flying around, some more wordy, and less comical, but this propaganda became ubiquitous in the neighborhood and, as of that morning, a hot commodity as no one had any of these items. At least in this group.

"Whoa. Where did you get those?" asked Mike.

"My brother. He went to the Nazi joint, and they gave 'em to him," explained Bullethead. "Now, what do you guys have?"

"I want to look at 'em first," said Randy Beecher.

"Ok, ok," said Bullethead, "I'll spread 'em out over here."

He walked over to Mr. Duffy's worktable and laid each item down, one by one. "But if any one of you mess them up, I'll smash your face in."

In a minute Bullethead had laid out his wares and watched like a hawk as the group approached the table and inspected his goods.

Weezer looked at his watch. He would have liked to get involved but he had to leave. The morning had somehow turned into early afternoon, and he had to go to work. He quickly glanced at the soon-to-be bargained-for items and left the garage. By now, the rain had stopped, and the sun was burning up the moisture in wispy vapor trails from the black-tarred streets.

That summer, Weezer started to deliver the Chicago American, a daily afternoon paper and, in a strictly metaphoric manner, said good-bye to all that was young and foolish. From here on he had to generate his own income and try to grasp and understand the mysteries of capitalism. Of course, he had no idea at the time that this would be the start of something that would dog him for the rest of his life, but it felt a little different to him, like big-boy stuff. When he was hired, he bought the mandatory canvas bag and installed metal hooks on the handlebars of his bike to hang the bag on.  He was assigned Route 10, which had 43 weekday papers starting at 69th Street and went to 74th Street, along the west side of Wolcott. Every weekday afternoon, he had to pick up his papers from Harry the Jew, who ran the branch out of a garage behind a Lithuanian restaurant at 69th and Artesian.

Harry was a tall, middle-aged man who seemed to be eternally tanned and whose bald spot on the top of his head was always smooth and shiny like polished river rock. Weezer couldn't tell if he was Jewish or not because Weezer had no idea what a Jew was supposed to look like. He didn't know any that he could think of, for his world at the time consisted of all Catholics and Publics and anything else was strictly a curiosity to be touched and poked at like a hands-on exhibit at the Museum of Science and Industry. He had always pictured Jews to look like Morey Amsterdam who played "Buddy" on the "Dick Van Dyke Show." Harry didn't look like Morey Amsterdam at all; for one thing his whole-body shape was different. Harry was tall and had a long face whereas Morey Amsterdam was a short oval-faced creature who always had a joke. Harry had no jokes. He was as serious as a heart-attack and ran a tight ship at the branch, always having one of his captains cleaning up around the place and keeping a close eye on the supply of rubber bands in the communal bin. God forbid if you took too many rubber bands to do your papers, "That shit cost money," Harry would say, and God strike you dead if he caught you shooting the rubber bands around the branch.

"You'll put someone's god damn eye out and then your parents will come looking to sue me," Harry would say.

There was a technique in rolling and banding the newspapers that Weezer had been working on that some of the other guys had down cold. In one Ninja-like move, the paper would find itself rolled, rubber banded and in the bag with the heavy end of the paper inserted first, as this made it easier to throw in one motion.

Not only did the newspapers have to be banded tightly but there were also aerodynamic conditions to be considered. The newspapers were delivered to each home by throwing them onto the porch while riding a bike down the sidewalk. To do this properly, one had to simultaneously calculate many things. There was the weight of the paper, the speed of the bike, the atmospheric conditions of the moment and other potential factors such as dogs chasing you or small children playing on the sidewalk. Throwing the papers on the larger porches that extended along the entire front of the house was a piece of cake; the real test was the small porch with the aluminum door. First, the target area was smaller, and you had the dreaded "big bang" factor. If you threw too hard, the paper would loudly hit the aluminum door. If they had a small dog, it promptly alerted the homeowner of the arrival of the afternoon paper in a "big bang" manner, often leaving a dent on the door.

That day, while riding to the branch, Weezer doubled up with Danny Wachenski. Danny lived two blocks from Weezer and had the route on the east side of Wolcott. While they did not travel in the same circles, Danny was a grade ahead of Weezer and a lot crazier, they would occasionally double-up on their routes, especially on winter Sunday mornings when it was still dark and scary out on the cold and vacant streets.

Behind his back, everyone called Danny "Sweatski" because he always seemed to be sweating. It was warm for spring that day and despite the sleeveless tee shirt he had on and his fresh flat-top haircut, which along with the rolled-up scapular around his neck made him look like a young grunt in a trench, the sweating seemed justified. Danny would have large beads of sweat along the top of his forehead in the middle of January or a wet upper lip in December and had to carry a handkerchief with him to constantly wipe his brow or lip. No one ever mentioned his sweating to him because he would probably crush your face if you did. He was a big and violent boy, and his nickname was one of those neighborhood in-jokes that you had to be careful who you said it around. Whenever Weezer saw Danny, he had to remind himself not to stare at or mention anything about the excessive moisture that would amass on Danny's face. Today was no different; a moist stripe was forming down the middle of his shirt like a surgical scar from a triple-bypass and would soon run down the entire length of his shirt by the time they got to the branch.

They rode silently in single file to the branch, wrapped their newspapers, and loaded their canvas bags onto the handlebars of their bikes. Weezer followed Danny out the narrow gangway that went through the pungent exhaust from the restaurant kitchen fan. He noticed that Danny now had an embryonic sweat mark starting down his back, which Weezer was sure would be a full-blown racing stripe by the time they got to their routes. Usually at this point they would start to peddle to their routes, but Danny, being in the front, held out his hand like a Calvary sergeant giving the halt order to his troops. Weezer stopped like a dutiful soldier.

Danny turned and looked at Weezer. While arching his eyebrows as high as they could go with an impish look on his face, he asked Weezer, "Do you want to stop by the Nazi joint?"

"Ok," he said. They rode the opposite way of their routes over to 71st Street, then down Rockwell. When they got there, they saw on the corner a typical brown two-story building that resembled every other building on the block, except this one had a large red Nazi flag hanging on the side of it. The flag, which covered at least a story and a half of the building, had a big white circle and black swastika dead in the middle. It seemed totally out of place.

At the Nazi headquarters Weezer figured he could load up on free collectibles that Bullethead had and do some heavy trading in Duffy's garage. Besides Bullethead's brother, no one that Weezer knew had been there yet, so anything he could get would probably fetch a high return.

The building had a hand-painted sign over the front entrance which formally declared it as "Rockwell Hall," which to Weezer seemed like an uninspired choice because every building on the thirty mile stretch of Rockwell Street could be named the same. Later he found out that it was named after the fallen Pseudo-Nazi commander who had been shot a couple of years before.

There were ten bikes parked outside the building. Apparently, this place was fast becoming either a hang-out or a one-time curiosity stop for the teen boys it seemed to attract. Weezer and Danny parked their bikes, which was difficult because of the forty-three folded copies of the Chicago American hanging off the front handlebars.

They passed under the "Rockwell Hall" sign and entered the building. Not knowing what to expect, Weezer tensed up. The whole Nazi thing had him a bit confused. Weren't they supposed to be the bad guys?

Weezer thought to himself: "what if this is all a trap and once inside, we're captured and forced into stalag camps, never to be seen again unless we doggedly tunnel our way out by using a small, sharpened eating utensil."

His fears abated when he saw about fifteen other guys his age and he figured there was safety in numbers. They couldn't capture all of them at once, could they?

Once inside they found themselves in a large storefront, which had a kind of pawn shop layout, with glass cases along the walls, each one displaying the wares of the vendor, in this case being Swastika armbands and buttons, blitzkrieg key chains, big-print versions of "Mein Kampf," and other such goodies. Some of the stuff was free, like the flyers and cartoons that blanketed the neighborhood. And Hitler was everywhere. The ever-present Fuhrer wafted over the entire room in the form of hanging pictures, pamphlets, books, and just plain dogma. Weezer milled about the room with the other guys. Everyone looked like wary tourists checking out the hand-made trinkets laid out by local merchants on a tropical island and when they spoke, it was in hushed tones, like they were at a museum.

It seemed new to everyone. The collective newbie feeling made Weezer ease a little bit because he did not want to be the new guy in a roomful of Nazis, as he was sure the hazing ritual was brutal.

Weezer reached through a crowd and took a couple of free hand-bills from a pile that lay on one of the counters and was about to inspect the other free stuff when Danny, who was now wearing a large swastika button on his shirt, tapped Weezer on the shoulder.

"Hey, come with me to the back," he said.

Weezer followed. Danny led him to the back room, which seemed like a regular office with cheap wood paneling, some book-shelves, and a used desk. Behind the desk sat what Weezer thought was a wax figure of Hitler without his mustache, but suddenly the figure's head moved slightly, and he realized this was a real person, decked out in head-to-toe Nazi. He was thin, almost frail, and had on a brown shirt with all the necessary patches, a dark tie, and a wide leather belt with a strap that went over his right shoulder. His hair was shiny and black and thinning and combed over just like Hitler's. In fact, except for the lack of moustache, this guy seemed to emulate Hitler in every way. Weezer wondered why he didn't do the moustache. Was it a medical thing, like, did he get a rash or something under his nose if he tried to grow one? He just guessed at the possible reasons. Maybe by not having it, he was expressing his individuality within Nazi circles, or maybe he always had one but just screwed it up shaving that morning and decided, "the hell with it, I'll just shave the damn thing off."

Flanked behind the faux Fuhrer, were what seemed to be his muscle. Two burly, blonde attendants with the same uniform, but with less patches and insignia, stood at attention behind the Fuhrer lite. Between them a Nazi flag hung on the wall, ostensibly to give an aura of officialism to the whole scene. A small spotlight shone down on where the leader sat, which highlighted the sheen of his hair and his receding hairline. He slowly scanned the office that was filling up with the young male crowd flowing in from the front part of the store. Apparently, the show was about to begin.

The crowd silently formed a semi-circle around the desk. They looked at the leader, and he returned the stare. His bottom jaw stuck out slightly looking somewhat menacing, as he did a slow pan back and forth with just his head moving, like an animatronic display at Nazi World or something. Weezer looked about the room to see how everyone else was reacting only to get the same looks in return from the other spectators, apparently with the same questions Weezer had. Finally fake Fuhrer stood up and did one more quick pass around the room, stopped and then rigidly raised his right arm three-quarters and yelled, "Heil Hitler!" The muscle behind him took the cue and responded loudly together, "Heil Hitler!"

The sudden burst of activity caught everyone by surprise and got their attention.

"White power!" he announced and paused for effect. Then he again scanned the room, allowing time for the premise of his speech to sink into each impressionable young, white, male mind. "White men must unite against the scourge that is the nigger and the Jew! They are what hold us down! The nigger wants your neighbor-hoods, wants your life, and wants to be like whitey!"

Weezer looked down at his feet and shuffled a bit.

"They need to stay on their side of town. We don't go there, and they don't come here. They want to march on Marquette Park, for what? To cause trouble. To be where they are not wanted?"

No one answered his rhetorical question.

"Marquette Park is for the white people and white people only! We don't go over to Washington Park or their parks, why do they want to come to ours?  Only to make trouble and rob you.  That's right, a whole parade of them will be marching down 71st Street.  Just imagine, the stores will all have to close for fear of these black bastards looting and robbing their businesses."

The intensity of his speech increased with each word.  He was approaching the end of his message when he paused again to let his point sink in while the rapt and silent audience returned his stare.  An uncomfortable silence fell about the room.

Weezer began to feel queasy and again shuffled his feet.  This was getting weird to him.  He felt his morning oatmeal slide around in his stomach and it was then that he let out a loud fart.  He didn't mean to, but it was one of those sneaky bastards that give you no advance warning so you could properly stifle it, like when you're in church or at the dinner table, it just came out.  The one good thing was that the attendees were all standing so close together that no one could identify the farting culprit.  Weezer looked about the room for the guilty party along with everyone else, hoping that such action would save him from any repercussions from the American Nazi Party.  He became concerned.  A few small snickers were quickly silenced when the head Nazi raised his arm and continued.

"This is serious shit!  Your parents have worked long and hard to make this neighborhood what it is today, and we cannot let it go to the dogs overnight!"

Even though Weezer was standing among a group of other guys, the Nazi seemed to be looking right at him.  Weezer was sure that the Nazi was thinking: "I know it was you, you little fucker, and you will die a horrible death."  But then the Nazi turned away and continued his speech.  Weezer glanced about the room searching for the exits, just in case.

"What can you do to help prevent this?" the Nazi continued, "a lot!  That's why we're here!  That's why we are giving these signs to you and your neighbors to let the niggers know that we do not want them here!  We do not appreciate their presence in our neighbor-hoods, and we need to let them know that!  For all that is right and holy!  White Power!  Heil Hitler!"

The muscle responded, "Heil Hitler!"

And the presentation was over.  The self-proclaimed Nazi leader exited the room through a side door to his left.  His muscle remained in Heil Hitler mode then followed him out through the same door.

Weezer felt that he had to get the hell out of there as fast as he could.  He was sure that Mr. Nazi would come after him with his goons.  Unfortunately, the murmuring crowd could only slowly file out of the room, which Weezer thought gave the Nazis plenty of time to go around the back of the building and meet him outside, where they would take him away in the back of a Nazi paddy wagon, never to be seen again.

After finally reaching the exit, Weezer stepped out and quickly looked around to see if they were waiting for him.  Much to his relief, he didn't see anyone in a Nazi uniform when Danny turned to him and said,

"Boy you're sweating like a pig."

Weezer felt his forehead and sure enough, the moisture was oozing out of his pores.  He wiped his hand on his pants and quickly stashed his collectibles into his bag as Danny and he got on their bikes to start their routes.

The farther away from the building they got, the better Weezer felt.  He became less fearful and more inquisitive.  As they rode away side-by-side Weezer turned to Danny and asked him, "What's the deal with the Nazis?"

"What do you mean?" answered Danny.

"I mean, weren't they the bad guys during World War Two?  Isn't that who we fought?"

"Oh, no man.  That was the German Nazis," Danny replied with an air of someone who knew about such things.

"They're different?" Weezer asked.

"Oh yeah, two different groups. These guys are different all together."

"How so?"

"Well, for one thing, these are American Nazis. Totally different from the German ones. These Nazis speak English, the Germans sure didn't. I think they bought the name or something."

It didn't sound right to Weezer and feeling a quick burst of defiance, he dared to question Danny's information. "Are you sure about that?"

With a glare, Danny turned to Weezer and sneered, "Are you calling me a liar?"

The combination of the look and the line drawn in the sand made Weezer back off.

"No, no, of course not," Weezer pussily replied, "It just seems a little strange, that's all."

Satisfied that the challenge to his keen insight had been extinguished, Danny tried to exude a mentor-like wisdom as he turned his attention back to the road.

"That it is, my man, that it is."

They rode in silence for the remaining three blocks of the ride, until they got to their routes.

Weezer rode down Wolcott tossing papers on porches and trying to reconcile the whole Nazi thing. It just didn't feel good in that place. There was a sense of stale air that permeated the small building. He could not put his finger on it at the time. It was a thick and heavy air that he did not want to breathe for fear of getting sick.

The idiot in the Hitler get-up reminded Weezer of a kid who outgrows Halloween but continues to trick-or-treat every year and gets strange looks from the people handing out candy at the door. He thought that most of the people in that room listening to him felt like candy-givers, which he knew he did, just staring at the pathetic figure who just didn't get it for some reason.

It was easy to deduce that Danny didn't know shit about the Nazis, yet he seemed enthralled with them as he paraded down 69th Street with the swastika buttons on his shirt. But then, everyone knew that Danny could be an idiot.

At the end of Weezer's route, he had no extra papers, which is good news, and all that remained in his bag were his Nazi collectibles. He rode back towards home. When he approached the corner of 73rd Street, he noticed the skull and crossbones and the "Nigger Beware" warning posted on the 'Stop' sign there. He stopped his bike and took a hard look at it. It wasn't the pirate-flag comic book skull and crossbones, but a 3D type, with artistic shading of the bony cheek and evil smile. It seemed to be copied from somewhere, like from a warning label on a bottle of cleaning solvent or some other deadly household product. Weezer remembered those labels used to scare the crap out of him when he was younger. It seemed like every bottle and box stored under the kitchen sink at home had the scary 3D skull and crossbones warning on it. It was enough to keep him from touching any of the containers for fear that he would get some of the deadly poison on his fingers and carelessly pick his nose or something and die a slow and painful death. He started to feel the same way about the propaganda in his bag.

He cut down the alley between Wolcott and Honore Streets, stopped at a garbage can and dumped the contents of his bag into it. This is stupid, he thought.

That night, after supper, he met the guys at Duffy's garage and had a trading session. For the price of only three Bardahl Men, he got five Woody-Woodpeckers, a large Pennzoil decal and a Tommy John card. It was a good night.

# CHAPTER 6

# HOLY NAME OUTING
## May 1970

On a beautiful summer evening in June, Father Tom Mallon looked at his watch as he stood outside the bright yellow school bus that sat idling in the parking lot of St. Justin's. The bus was loaded with altar boys and a few chaperones from the Holy Name Society for an outing to a Chicago White Sox game. Father Mallon and Father Cummins would accompany the attendees, courtesy of the Holy Name Society, as some sort of official spiritual escort. However, Father Mallon did not feel official in any sense of the word. He enjoyed going to the ballpark and had been looking forward to this evening.

Father Cummins, on the other hand, approached the waiting bus like a man walking towards the gallows. A slow and methodical pace gave away his attitude towards the evening's festivities. Father Cummins was a large man on the verge of losing the battle of the bulge and despite the warm summer evening ahead, he had on his full priest garb, black shirt, white collar, and black blazer. He had a graceful head of silver hair that swept straight back like an aging hipster and wore a constant grizzled look on his face that expressed his concern that the whole world was turning to shit and that only he carried the burden to save it.

"Ready to go Father Cummins?  You sure you need the jacket?  It's going to be a nice evening," asked Father Mallon as he approached the bus.

"You never know about the weather, right?  Let's just get this thing over with," said Father Cummins.

Mallon sensed that there was something on Cummins' mind. They had watched many baseball games together, both live and on TV.  He knew the priest was a big fan.

"Why the long face?  It should be a fun night tonight," asked Mallon.

"Oh nothing.  Just one of my moods, I guess.  Let's go."

They got on the bus and found their seats.  Danny Wachenski's father, a representative from Holy Name stood up to speak.

"Okay, okay.  Hear me out for a second," he said.  The noise on the bus simmered down and the passengers directed their attention to him.

"We should get to the park a little bit before game time.  We need to keep together so they can do a head count at the gate.  Okay? After that you can go where you want.  All the seats are together but remember, this bus will be leaving after the ninth inning, so after the game, meet at the same gate for a head count on the way out. Everyone got that?"

Everyone nodded or mumbled "yes" to Mr. Wachenski's satisfaction.  "Okay now, everyone have fun tonight," he said.  The bus pulled out of the school parking lot.

As the driver geared up to cruising speed, the passengers began singing a loud chorus of "*99 Bottles of Beer On the Wall*," the anthem for school outings.  They drove east on 71st Street to the

Dan Ryan Expressway, and then north to White Sox Park, about a half-hour ride.

"Ninety-nine bottles of beer on the wall, take one down and pass it around, ninety-eight bottles of beer on the wall." The repetitive song was supposed to go on ad nauseum until it reached one bottle of beer on the wall, but it never did. Either the bus would arrive at its destination before the song got to that final stanza or the kids would lose enthusiasm at about the seventy-fifth bottle of beer on the wall, where the song would fade to one or two voices that were eventually told to shut up by anyone within earshot.

Father Mallon felt that there could be other songs for the kids to sing without alcoholic beverages, but it kept twenty-five kids busy on the bus ride so he would have to put up with it.

The trip down 71st Street exposed the boys to a whole different world. A world of three-flats, corner groceries and black people. The sight of the entire black community amassed in one area of the city was an event for some of the boys who would stare in curiosity while others, usually the older boys who had been on this trip before, would yell out the window, "Hey Leroy!", to any black person they would see walking by.

This behavior did not sit well with Father Cummins. He almost cuffed Mike Raskin for yelling out the window during the last trip. He was determined that there would not be any juvenile acts on this ride.

Cummins turned to Mallon, "When we get to the ballpark, I need to have a quick chat with you."

"Sure. Why not now?"

"Can't right now, gotta keep an eye on these kids. I don't want to get interrupted, which I know I will."

"Ok. Sure. At the ballpark then," Mallon responded. "Is it anything big? Should I be concerned about anything?"

"No, no. We'll straighten it out. Just a change in some procedures, that's all."

Just then, a loud voice was heard yelling out of one of the rear windows towards a middle-age black man walking down the street.

"Hey Leroy! Your momma calling you!" The bus exploded in laughter.

An angry Father Cummins rose and turned towards the source of the yelling.

"Be right back," he said to Father Mallon.

"Alright! Who's got the big mouth?" he said as he stormed down the aisle. Making his way towards the back rows of the bus, he immediately saw Mike Raskin and determined that he was the source of the yelling. He exploded on Mike. "Mr. Raskin, didn't you learn anything from the last trip?"

Before Mike could plead his innocence, Mr. Burton, a chaperone, who was sitting directly behind Mike said "Sorry, Father. Just kind of slipped out I guess."

Stunned, Father Cummins gave him an incredulous glare, shook his head, and quickly returned to his seat. He turned to Father Mallon.

"These kids are fucked, cause their parents are fucked," he said as he reached into his jacket and pulled out a flask. He unscrewed the cap and took a long drink. He turned back to Mallon and offered the flask to him.

"Want a snort?"

"No, no. I'm good."

Cummins screwed the cap back on and put the flask back into his jacket.

After a short ride on the Dan Ryan Expressway, the bus arrived at the ballpark and pulled into a parking lot. The passengers exited from the bus and headed for Gate 5. At the head of the crowd approaching the entrance gate, was Mr. Wachenski. The spiffily clad Andy Frain usher, in his blue uniform with gold piping on the sleeves, a peaked hat with a white visor and starchy white gloves, accepted a stack of tickets from Mr. Wachenski. The usher counted the heads. Apparently, the ticket and head count matched, so the group was allowed into the park and up a set of endless ramps that led to their seats, the first ten rows in the upper deck along the third base line.

They settled into their seats when the first group of boys decided to walk around the park. Danny Wachenski, Mike Raskin and Weezer O'Donnell got up from their seats to start off for the great exploration of the ballpark.

"Where are you guys headed?" Mr. Wachenski asked the boys.

His son, Danny replied, "Lower Deck. See if we can get some foul balls."

"Okay, but don't be gone all game, alright? Check back in once in a while."

Danny rapidly nodded his head. "Okay, Dad. Bye."

And the three of them were off.

Cummins and Mallon sat off the aisle. The remaining kids and chaperones were scattered about the section that was allotted. Mr. Burton, who was sitting three rows ahead of the priests, rose from his seat and started up the aisle ostensibly to go to the beer stand. He stopped at the row where Cummins and Mallon sat.

"Hey Father Cummins. Sorry about that back on the bus. Can I buy you a beer?"

Cummins gave Burton a hard stare. "I suppose. But your penance is that you buy Father Mallon one also."

"Sure, sure, Father. Be right back," a visibly relieved Burton said and went up the aisle to the beer stand.

The priests sat back in silence and watched the Boston Red Sox, in their road gray uniforms, doing their pregame batting practice on the field. Despite it still being light out, the ballpark lights were on which, with the setting sun, gave the park an unnatural glow. An occasional shout from a vendor would rise above the hum of the pregame crowd.

"Hot Dogs!  Hot Dogs!  Get your red hots here!"

"Souvenirs!  Souvenirs!"

"Beer!  Ice cold Beer!"

Andy the Clown, a staple at the ballpark, yelled from the lower deck, "LETS GO YOU WHITE SOX!" Mallon looked down at Andy along the first base line.  He was easy to pick out.  He wore a white clown outfit with red polka dots, a red derby and a nose that lit up on his painted white face.  Another clue of his whereabouts was the small crowd of children that followed him around the ballpark and beseeched him to light up his nose and make animal figures from balloons.

The sound and visuals captured their reverence for the game as they grinned and stared down at the field.  The only visual flaw was the different shades of green on the field.  For whatever reason, the team thought that having a lighter color artificial turf infield and an outfield of regular grass, which was a darker shade, was a good idea.

Mallon spoke out loud to no one in particular.  "God, I love this."

Cummins nodded in agreement as he pulled the flask out from his jacket, took a drink, capped it, and put it back.

"Except they screwed it up with this infield," Cummins replied.

"Yeah, you're right about that." Mallon said.  "I remember when my Uncle Wally took me to my first game here.  I saw Billy Pierce beat Bob Feller. 1952.  It was a sloppy game, lots of errors, but, hell, it was Bob Feller.  You beat him anyway you could."

Cummins nodded and, in preparation for what he was about to say, drew his flask out again and took another sip.  "I knew your Uncle Wally."

"Really?" Mallon said, obviously surprised.

"Yeah. I knew your uncle. I knew him well. He was a member of my 'Lost Boys' club."

"Lost Boys club? What was that all about."

"Well, when I first got here, I was young and stupid, thought I could change the world. Or at least one member of the Lost Boys club. That was the goal, anyway. The Lost Boys club was a group of unsavory but salvageable, or so I thought, characters that I focused on. Try to get them in church occasionally. Turn them around, even a little bit. Maybe at least show them an alternative path. Whatever I could do to at least give them a shot."

"Did it work?"

"Hell no, most of them died violently. Like your uncle."

"You know about that?"

"Oh, yeah. It was a big to-do for at least a couple of weeks back then. But I'll tell you, I wasn't surprised given his line of work." Cummins paused and looked as if he were debating whether to say his next sentence. "I was there the night he passed, at the hospital."

"You gave him his Last Rights?" Mallon asked.

"Yes. I was there." Cummins paused and turned to Mallon. "You were involved with him for a while, weren't you? You and that Gallagher kid?"

Mallon was caught off-guard and let out a small cough before he answered. "Yeah, a very little bit in my errant days of youth. Very miniscule stuff. After all, he was my guardian."

"Yeah, I know. I'm sorry about your parents passing."

"Thank you," said Mallon. "Mom got hit by a truck and Dad died from the hazards of the business he was in. Or so I was told."

"Is there any doubt in your mind?"

"I suppose, but I don't think about it much. Not anymore. Doesn't matter anyway."

"No, it doesn't," said Cummins. "Do you still see Gallagher? I've heard that he's now walking around in Wally's shoes. You know that right?"

"I went golfing with him a couple of weeks ago. Ran into him at the Jewels. As a matter of fact, I'm golfing with him again this Sunday. I'm aware that Freddy Gallagher is no saint, but believe me, Wally's shoes weren't that big."

"Big enough. Look Father Mallon, Tom, just be careful, that's all. Watch yourself. Gallagher is bad news. Real bad news. He belongs in your Lost Boys club. Mine is full."

Mallon paused to consider what Cummins was trying to tell him before he responded.

"I'll take that snort now," was all he could come up with.

Cummins reached into his jacket and pulled out his flask, uncapped it, and handed it to Mallon who took a long hard sip. He handed it back to Cummins just as Burton came back with the beers.

"Here you go Fathers."

"Thank you," said Mallon.

Father Cummins waived the sign of the cross at Burton and said, "I want you to say five Hail Mary's while we're here also."

"But I bought you the beer," said Burton.

"Your sin was particularly egregious Mr. Burton. You did it in front of the kids."

"Alright Father. You're right. I'll do 'em now."

"Before you drink that beer," ordered Father Cummins.

"Yes Father." Burton quickly bowed his head and went down to his seat and put his cup of beer on the ground. He turned back to Father Cummins who glowered at him to start his penance. Mr. Burton turned away, bowed his head, and started reciting the five Hail Mary's.

A smiling Father Mallon turned to Father Cummins.  "Beer and Hail Mary's for penance?  What was that all about?"

"Burton is an asshole.  He deserves it," said a grinning Father Cummins.

He took a sip of his beer and got serious.

"Tom, I need to talk to you about the parish finances."

"Ok.  I'm listening."

"We were short last month in the weekly offerings."

"And I am somehow responsible?" asked Mallon.

"I'm not saying that, Tom.  I am aware of your past with Wally, and that Gallagher kid, and I do not want to chance anything.  It just doesn't look good."

Cummins took a sip of his beer.  "I'm doing this to cover both of our asses."

"Doing what?"

"As of this week, Father Burke will be responsible for the gathering and depositing of the offerings."

Father Mallon turned and blankly stared at the field.

Cummins took another long sip of his beer, leaned over close to Mallon's ear, and softly said, "I know about your prior stint at St. Alphonse.  What the hell happened there?  How can a parish Las Vegas Night lose over five hundred dollars?"

Mallon turned with a look of surprise, as if an age-old family secret had been divulged.

"Yeah, yeah.  I know about it." Cummins said.  "I'm told that it's the only Las Vegas Night ever to lose money in the history of the Archdiocese of Chicago.  Listen, Tom, you're a bit old for a babysitter, and I'm too old to be one.  They tell me I gotta keep an eye on you but to hell with that.  Look me in the eye."

Mallon closed his mouth and obeyed.

"You are done with this gambling stuff," Cummins said. "The dice, the horses, the sports betting, all of it. You're done. Can we agree on that?"

Mallon looked Cummins in the eye and said, "Yes. It's all over. All of it. You won't have any problems from me."

"Good, good. Now let's watch the game."

* * * * * * *

Danny, Weezer and Mike made it down to the lower deck, left of the visitor's dugout to get close to pregame batting practice. The Red Sox were spraying baseballs all over the field. Weezer watched closely at each player's swing, thinking that he could improve his game by visual osmosis. Of the three, Weezer was the baseball fan. He had a baseball card collection, read the box scores every morning and could recite the top ten batting average leaders by memory. Danny and Mike could not care less about stats, standings, or league leaders, but they both enjoyed the surroundings and the setting.

The Boston players lined up to take their cuts in the temporary batting cage that was placed around home plate during the pre-game warmups. Each player took about ten swings. As one player entered the cage, another would pop out of the dugout to await his turn in the cage.

A Boston player with the number 8 on his back came out of the dugout. Danny turned to Weezer. "Who's that? Number 8. What's his name?"

"That's Carl Yastrzemski, man."

"Is he any good?"

"Yeah, he's real good."

Danny turned back to the field and yelled to Yastrzemski.

"Hey, Yastrzemski, you suck!"

The future Hall of Famer, with his bat on his shoulder, turned around and smiled at Danny.

"Hey, did you see that? He turned around and looked at me," said Danny.

"Yeah, he did," said an unimpressed Weezer.

Danny pointed to another Boston player. "Who's that?"

"Tony Conigliaro," said Weezer.

"Is he any good?"

"Yeah, he's good."

"Hey..." Danny's voice trailed off. He turned back to Weezer. "What's his name again?"

"Conigliaro. Tony Conigliaro."

"Say it one more time."

Weezer's exasperation was evident. "Conigliaro. Con-eeg-lee-arrow."

"Hey Con-eeg-lee-arrow! You suck!" yelled Danny to the confused ballplayer.

Just then, an Andy Frain usher tapped Danny on the shoulder.

"Can I see your tickets?"

Instead of complying and pleading ignorance of where their real seats were, the three boys ran up the aisle, found an exit and ran to the concession area that wrapped around the ballpark underneath the stands.

The concession area was a bustling walk-around tunnel that ran beneath the stands and was lined with souvenir and food stands, bathroom exits and entrances, and administrative areas. Its old Chicago Brick walls hid under layers of white paint and blown-up photos of the team in action over the years. The delicious aroma of grilled onions wafted about the area and a layer of cigarette smoke lingered over everyone and everything. On hot summer evenings, like that night, everyone perspired, which added to the blend of exotic aromas. It was a kaleidoscope of the senses for the three boys as they walked amid the crowd that contributed to the carnival type atmosphere.

Weezer liked watching the people. There were couples on dates, families, groups of boys and girls by themselves, old wrinkly men in straw hats slowly walking alone and occasionally, Weezer remembered seeing groups of nuns. Italians, Greeks, Germans, all the white folk, black people, Spanish people. Young and old. These were people that Weezer didn't see in his neighborhood. And he was curious about the different people and their stories. He wanted to walk up to the old man in the straw hat and ask him, where was he from? Why was he there by himself? Where'd he get the hat? The only thing that compared to this was downtown.

Weezer and Mike had taken some bus trips downtown and walked around in awe amid the tall buildings. On certain hot days, downtown could smell like piss, there weren't any grilled onions to mask the smell. On occasion, the distinct and pungent stock yard aroma would make its presence known at the ballpark, which Weezer didn't mind. He had long ago decided that he liked the smell of death better than the smell of piss.

"I'm thirsty," said Mike. "I'm getting some pop."

"Okay. I can use a drink myself," said Weezer.

Wayne got in line for the concession stand and Weezer followed. He turned to Danny.

"You getting one?"

"No. I'm good. I'll wait here," said Danny as he pointed to the wall behind him.

Weezer watched him as Danny leaned against the wall next to a concession vender who was focused on counting a wad of dollar bills he held in his hand. The goods that he sold, large wispy clouds of cotton candy attached to a paper cone wrapped in plastic, were propped against the wall next to him, each attached to a large pegboard that the vendor used to carry his wares into the stands. Weezer winced as he became aware of what Danny was up to.

Danny, thinking that he was slick, nonchalantly grabbed one of the cotton candies from the board and started to walk away. The vendor looked up from his counting, turned to Danny and then back to his money, finished the count, folded the money, put it in his pocket and then grabbed Danny by the neck of his shirt.

"Hey pal. Where do you think you're going?" the vendor said.

Weezer did not hear Danny's explanation as he watched the vendor attract a security guards' attention and hand Danny over to him. They both disappeared into the crowd.

Mike turned around from the concession stand with his coke in hand and Weezer stepped up in line to make his order. He also received his cup of ice-cold pop, saw Mike waiting by where Danny had previously stood, and walked over to him. Mike looked about for Danny.

"Did you see where Danny went?" Mike asked Weezer.

"Sweatski got busted. Tried to swipe some cotton candy. The dicks took him away."

Mike shrugged at the inevitability. "Oh well. Let's go up and watch the game."

"Yeah," said Weezer. "The starting lineups should be up on the scoreboard."

* * * * * * * *

Father Cummins was copying the starting lineups from the scoreboard onto his scorecard.  "They're going with Joel Horlen tonight. I don't know how much that guy has left," he said.

Mallon nodded and said, "Oh to be over the hill at the ripe old age of 33."

Cummins was focusing more on the game now.  His absolutions and admonishments were finished for the evening.  He said what he had to say to Father Mallon and felt comfortable that he had dealt with the situation.  He knew of Mallon's past, both before and after he became a priest, and believed that he had nipped it in the bud.

 He also received a free beer from Burton.  He could relax now and focus on the game.

The game started well for the White Sox as they got out to a 5-0 lead after three innings and Cummins' attitude paralleled the score. He emptied his flask by the third inning taking a drink for every Sox run and was prepared to make it through the rest of the game on a steady routine of a beer every other inning.  Plans of great men can go awry.

In the top of the fourth inning, the White Sox third baseman, Bill Melton, committed an error that allowed the Red Sox to score three unearned runs.  Cummins rose from his seat and yelled in the general direction of Melton, "They got rid of Pete Ward for you? Jeez!"

As Cummins sat back down, a security guard came down the aisle and stopped at the row where Mr. Wachenski sat, leaned over, and spoke in his ear.  Wachenski turned around and saw his son, Danny, standing next to another security guard at the top of the aisle.  He then rose and followed the original security guard up the stairs.

This does not look good, thought Father Mallon as he and the entire section watched the scene unfold before them.

Wachenski was listening to the security guard, who occasionally pointed to Danny as he told his story.

"Aw, shit.  What did the kid do now?" Cummins said.

"It does not look good," replied Mallon.

Wachenski bobbed his head in agreement with the guards who then left Danny with his clearly irate father.  Wachenski looked down upon the curious eyes of their group who witnessed his public embarrassment. He grabbed Danny by the neck and disappeared.

Meanwhile, Weezer and Mike had long finished their pops. After tearing out the bottoms of the cups, they were now using them as megaphones while they slowly made their way up the ramps to the upper deck and their seats.

"Extra! Extra! Read all about it! Gary O'Donnell is a pud!" yelled Mike.

"Extra! Extra! Mike Raskin has no dick! He's a dickless Raskin!" yelled Weezer in response to Mike's original news flash.

Neither loud pronouncement was heard by anyone other than the two orators, as the crowd was thin that night and there was no one else on the ramps. The sparse crowd gave the boys, they thought, the license to be extra silly with their news bulletins.

"Raskin's never touched a tit! Film at ten!"

"Except your mother's tit!" yelled Mike.

A line had been crossed and Weezer lunged at Mike in only a partial playful manner. Weezer knew he could take Mike, so he had to let him know who was the boss. He swiftly turned Mike around and got him in a full nelson.

"Take it back!"

"Fuck you!!" responded Mike.

"Take it back!" continued Weezer.

Then from below the ramp a loud authoritative voice emanated in their direction.

"Hey you guys! Knock it off up there!"

Quickly both boys scampered up the ramps and did not stop until they had reached the top. Out of breath, the two boys stopped at the top of their section.

"I gotta piss," said Mike.

"Me too," replied Weezer.

Together they walked into the men's room and approached the twenty-foot-long trough that served as a communal urinal. There was a sign above it that said, "For Future White Sox Players Only." As the boys relieved themselves, Weezer looked up at the sign.

"I guess this means I'm going to be playing for the Sox when I grow up."

Mike let out a snort and then immediately came a loud bang from inside one of the stalls. A loud voice followed the loud bang.

"A fucking cotton candy? You got caught swiping a fucking cotton candy? What the hell is wrong with you?"

And then quickly there was another bang. A double bang. The sound of skin on skin, a slap, and then the sound of something hitting the wall.

"Look at me! If you ever put me in this position again, I swear I will knock you into the middle of next week! Do you understand?"

"Yes, sir," was the meek reply.

Weezer and Mike both realized who the parties were in the stall. Weezer mouthed the word "Sweatski" and both the boys zipped up and quietly slipped out from the restroom.

As Weezer and Mike walked past Father Mallon towards their seats, he motioned for them to come to him. They nervously looked at each other and obliged.

"Hey guys, what happened with Daniel?"

Weezer spoke first. "Don't know Father. We lost him downstairs."

Mike nodded in quick agreement.

"Ok. You can go to your seats now."

Mallon watched as the boys walked down about three rows and took seats next to each other.

"You know they're not going to tell you anything, right?" said Cummins.

"Yes, I know.  But sometimes it's what they don't say that tells you a lot," said Mallon.

"Did you learn anything from what they didn't say?"

"Nothing at all.  Not a thing."

As they took their seats, Mike turned to Weezer, "You know you're going to hell for lying to a priest."

"I didn't lie.  We did lose him, and I don't know what happened to him.  So, fuck you."

"Okay, I'll buy it."

Mike turned around and tugged Weezer's shirt sleeve.  Weezer turned and they both watched as Danny made his way down the aisle with his father a couple steps behind him.  Danny had a morose demeaner and looked down as he descended the aisle.  He came to their row and sat next to Weezer.  His cheeks were red, and his eyes were swollen with tears and pain.  There was also a small red bruise on his right temple.

"You okay, man?"

Danny did not say anything but just nodded.

Fathers Mallon and Cummins, and the rest of the group watched the small, sad parade as it came down the aisle.  Mr. Wachenski sat in his seat with the other dads and acted as if nothing had happened.  Business as usual.

"So, what did I miss here?  Sox are up five-three?  Good deal.  Where's the beer guy at?" he said to no one in particular, but certainly loud enough for everyone to hear.

Cummins leaned over to Mallon.  "I said it once, I'll say it again.  These kids are fucked."

Mallon gave him a grim look.  His eyes said, 'no, that can't be.'

Cummins nodded back, "Oh yes it is."

The uncomfortable awkwardness in the group began to wane after a couple of innings of horrible baseball by the White Sox.

They had committed two errors leading to Boston scoring four runs and the once seemingly insurmountable five run lead was now down to one. The group now had far more serious issues than what Wachenski did to his kid.

As the game went on, Weezer tried making small talk with Danny who said nothing but nod his head or grunt something that resembled a word a couple of times. Finally, Weezer decided to go for broke.

"Want to go have a smoke?"

Danny's eyes widened and he turned around. His father was still sitting three rows up.

He responded in a disappointed tone, "No, you guys go."

Weezer and Mike looked at each other and shrugged with their eyebrows and then both headed up the aisle.

They got halfway down the exit ramp and looked around. There was no one around. Mike pulled out his rumpled pack of Kents and took a cigarette from the pack. Weezer lit a match and Mike took the first drag and handed it to Weezer, who also took a drag and held on to the smoke.

"Man, I'm glad my old man don't smack me around like that," said Weezer as he exhaled.

"Me too. Sometimes I'm glad not to have an old man," said Mike.

Weezer contemplated Mike's response, took another drag from the cigarette and gave it back to Mike.

"Does your old lady ever hit you?"

"She used to when I was smaller. But now I just kinda laugh when she does. I probably shouldn't, she just gets madder and tries harder. But I just can't help it sometimes. She makes this scrunched up face when she tries to hit me."

Mike scrunched his face in a pale imitation and took a drag from the smoke. Weezer was starting to laugh at Mike's imitation when they both saw Mr. Burton coming down the ramp in their direction. Mike held the still lit cigarette behind his back as both boys froze in Burton's presence.

"Good game, huh guys? By the way, that stuff will stunt your growth." He walked past the boys and continued down the ramp.

Weezer and Mike looked at each other in relief as Weezer grabbed the cigarette and took a final drag. "Come on, let's get back up there."

The dark of night surrounded the illuminated ballpark as a haze of smoke amassed above the field like a hovering spacecraft. Weezer and Mike arrived back in their section and found the aisle congested with younger kids and Andy the Clown. Andy was turning his lighted nose on and off while making unrecognizable animals from balloons he had in his pocket.

Just then, the sound of a loud crack of a bat hitting a ball grabbed everyone's attention. It was a sharply hit ball to the White Sox third baseman, who let the ball go through his legs into left field.

A now tipsy Father Cummins excitedly rose from his seat and yelled at the field, "Melton, you're a bum!" As he finished his pronouncement, he lost his balance and fell on Andy the Clown who promptly fell on Father Mallon, who was still sitting in his seat. A surprised Father Mallon tried to brace for the falling oncoming clown, but Andy was on him before he could properly protect himself. Mallon's head made heavy contact with the metal armrest of the seat.

The idyllic vision of the baseball diamond left Father Mallon's head. It was replaced by darkness that slowly lit up to reveal him kneeling before his father's coffin.

He would have been ten years old. Mallon had done the math hundreds of times in his head. This was important to him. One's age at the time of the event can go far towards the credibility of one's memories. He smelled the scent of McFee's Funeral Parlor on

Western. It was more than just clusters of dying flowers crowded around his father's open casket. There was a distinct sceptic undertone with hints of over-done coffee and cigarette smoke that mingled together to form the unique aroma. The wake was held for three days. Every night friends, family and acquaintances would dress up like they were about to attend a somber wedding, greet Catherine and then sit down for the next three hours, drink bad coffee and talk about the same things with the same people that they had talked to the night before.

Tommy knelt before Richard's open casket and started an Our Father. He snuck a peak at the figure in the casket that was supposed to be his father, a figure dressed in a suit and tie with hands neatly folded upon his oddly flat stomach with a rosary wrapped around them like spiritual handcuffs. His hair was neatly combed, which was Tommy's first clue that something was amiss. And his skin was a deep peach, almost orange. Didn't anyone else see that? His father had rough-hewn, pale skin and an unruly auburn mane that only had a sense of order when he ran his right hand through it.

"Our Father, who art in Heaven, hallowed be thy name. Thy kingdom come; thy will be done on earth as it is in heaven."

Tommy stopped his prayer. He quizzically turned his head as he again stared at the father figure in the casket. The jowls of his cheeks overlapped the collar of his shirt. He never recalled his father having jowls, nor for that matter a shirt with a collar. Something was just not right. Something was off. He looked at the eyes. They were closed, which made him look like he was asleep. At the bottom of the eyelids, above the lashes, a small ridge of makeup had built up which made him recoil in confusion as he realized that his father's face was behind a coating of makeup. He closed his eyes and continued the prayer.

"Give us this day our daily bread, forgive us our trespasses, as we forgive them who have trespassed against us."

He stopped and looked at his father. Suddenly, both of his father's eyes opened and a small smile sent wee pebbles of makeup dropping to the collar of his shirt. His father winked at him, closed his eyes and was dead again.

Tommy declined to finish the prayer, quickly made the sign of the cross, stood up and looked for his mother, Catherine. She was standing at the side of the room, against a flowery backdrop talking with Uncle Wally, her brother.

Uncle Wally was generally clad in a short-sleeve summer shirt and a baggy pair of Levi's, but tonight he had on his only suit with a red checkered tie, but he still looked the same to Tommy. Uncle Wally looked at Tommy and smiled. Suddenly, a fully grown Freddy Gallagher appeared from behind Uncle Wally and came after Tommy.

Without realizing why he was running, Tommy took off with Freddy chasing him. Tommy ran, where he did not know. It was dark like the night. There was a small speck of light ahead of him. He ran for it. He dared not look back at Freddy as he feared he would gain on him. The light was coming from behind a doorway that had a large cross hanging over it. Suddenly, Catherine appeared in front of the door. She had a bright halo above her head, and she smiled at him. She turned and opened the door. With a soft wave of her hand, she motioned him to enter. The light got brighter. Tommy continued to follow the light.

Father Mallon opened his eyes and found himself face to face with Andy the Clown and his illuminated nose.

"Hey Father, are you okay? Hey Father," said Andy.

Father Mallon blinked a couple of times and managed to make a response.

"Yeah, yeah. I'm okay," he groggily replied.

"Sorry about that Father. I couldn't help it," said Andy.

Father Cummins' face appeared behind Andy's.

"It was my fault, Tom. I got a little bit excited. That damn Melton."

"That's okay. How long was I out?"

"Oh, maybe a couple of seconds," said Father Cummins.

Father Mallon rose from his seat and straightened his clothes. "I'm okay. I'm okay. Just let me sit down for a bit."

The small crowd gave way to allow Father Mallon to reclaim his seat. They slowly dispersed once it was established that he was alright.

"Are you sure you're alright Father?" said Andy.

"Yeah, yeah. I'm good Andy. You can go your way now."

"Thank you, Father. I'm so sorry."

"Not your fault Andy," said Father Cummins now sitting next to Father Mallon.

"Thank you, Father. Well enjoy the rest of the game."

"We will, Andy," said Father Cummins.

The Red Sox scored two in the ninth to win the game, 6-5. The loss made the ride home a sedate affair. Father Mallon sat quietly staring out the window as the grit of nighttime Chicago passed. Father Cummins' tilted, sleeping head lay on Father Mallon's shoulder for almost the entire ride home. As the bus pulled into St. Justin's parking lot, Father Cummins awoke, sat up, wiped a bit of drool from the side of his mouth and acted as if he was awake for the entire trip.

After the bus emptied and everyone went home. Cummins and Mallon entered the Rectory together and walked up the stairs to their rooms.

"Well, good night, Tom," said Cummins. "Are you feeling alright?"

"Yes, I am. As well as I can be after a Sox loss. I'll probably have a bit of a headache in the morning, but I should be fine. Good night, Father Cummins," replied Mallon.

Cummins strolled down the hall to his room and stopped just before he entered.  He turned to Mallon.

"Oh, and please don't forget about what we talked about earlier."

"You have my word," said Mallon.

"G'night," said Cummins as he entered his room.

Mallon entered his room, sat on the chair at his desk.  He went over the evening in his mind.  The ballgame.  The bus ride.  Father Cummins conversation.  He rose from his chair and pulled a piece of paper from his pants pocket and looked at it.

The betting slip he got from Freddy Gallagher showed that Mallon had bet against the Sox and won twenty-five dollars.  He smiled and let it be at that.

# CHAPTER 7

# WEEZER, MIKE, AND O'BRIEN June 1970

Rather than undo the many buttons down the front of his cassock, Father Mallon quickly pulled it over the top of his head and tossed it into a wooden box that served as a hamper, revealing the pink polo shirt he had on underneath.  He ran his hand over his head to smooth the hair that remained on his head, and quickly waved good-bye as he darted from the sacristy.

The hurried pace of Father Mallon during the closing procession of the mass confirmed to the three altar boys that walked alongside of him that he had a tee time that must be met or there would be hell to pay.

The 12:30 Mass was the last on Sundays and the church complex emptied out when it was over, especially during the summer when the school was closed.

Mike Raskins and Gary "Weezer" O'Donnell were in the altar boy section of the sacristy as they waved at Father Mallon.

"See ya, Father."

"Yeah, see ya, Father."

The boys quickly removed their cassocks and threw the bundled mass into the corner of the room.  Weezer opened the exit door and peered into the hallway, looked about both ways and then turned back to Mike.

"Nobody."

The altar boy's room in the sacristy was connected to the priest's area by a hallway that ran behind the altar itself.  The layout was the same, but the priest's room had a sink and finer crafted cabinetry.  Above the sink was the wine cabinet, which on occasion would hold an open bottle, which was why the first thing Weezer did when he entered the room was to check the cabinet only to find that all the bottles were sealed.

"Crap.  Nothing."

Also in the priest's room was a fabric-lined wicker basket, the size of a medium trash can, that was three-quarters filled with envelopes and cash, the collection results of the 12:30 Mass.  Mike and Weezer stared at the basket and then slowly turned toward each other.

"You sure about this?" Mike said to Weezer.

"Are you chickening out?"

"No, but this is straight-to-hell stuff that we're about to do, you know that right?"

"Only if you get caught," replied Weezer as he reached into the basket and grabbed a handful of cash and envelopes and stuffed them down the front of his pants.  He saw Mike's apprehension.  "Come on pussy.  Grab some."

Mike reached into the basket and removed his own wad of envelopes and cash.  "Now what?"

"Stuff 'em down your pants, idiot.  You don't want anyone seeing you leaving with that shit in your hands."

Mike obeyed and started to stuff the haul in his pants.  Sean O'Brien, the third altar boy, walked into the room.  He saw what was going on.  His expression was the same as if he had walked in on his parents having sex.  His eyes widened to maniacal widths, and he put both of his open palms over his mouth.

Everyone in the room froze.  Weezer and Mike realized they had been caught red-handed stealing money from the church by the biggest holy roller in the whole school.  Sean O'Brien was every nun's dream.  His knowledge of the catechism was legendary as was his rosary being a couple of beads short of a novation.  Sean was known as being a bit "slow."  Word in the neighborhood was that this was the result of his knack for being hit by automobiles.  Four times in the past six years Sean was hit by a car.  None of his physical injuries were severe, a stitch or two here and there, but each time he also incurred some head trauma, and it became evident over time that his mental faculties were not what they should be. He could recite bible verses to no end, but he had a tough time crossing streets.  Weezer was aware of this.

"Sean, it's not what you think," said Weezer.

O'Brien did not move.  He kept the frozen expression on his face as if he turned around for one final look at Gomorrah and became a pillar of salt.

"Sean.  Sean, are you alright?" Weezer asked.

O'Brien finally moved and slowly nodded his head while keeping his hands over his mouth.  Like an inopportune witness to a brutal murder scene, he kept himself from screaming at what he had just seen.

"What are you doing here anyway?" Weezer quizzed.

Without moving his hands from his mouth, O'Brien answered, "I came for the basket.  Father Mallon asked me to get it and bring it to the rectory since he was leaving early."

"How come you're just getting it now?" asked Weezer, aghast that O'Brien had ruined his heist.

O'Brien slowly pulled his hands down from his mouth. "I ran to the convent to get my rosary from Sister Judith. She went to Rome over the summer and had it blessed by Pope Paul, you know." He reached into his shirt pocket and pulled the rosary out and held it up as if he had caught a blue gill at Marquette Park.

"Pope Paul blessed that rosary?" asked Mike.

"Yep," beamed O'Brien.

For a moment, both Mike and O'Brien stared in silent awe at the dangling set of beads as if it was a pocket-watch swung by a hypnotist. The lull allowed Weezer to formulate a plan.

"Sean, you know that Pope Paul is a member, right?" said Weezer.

Weezer's question broke the trance and caught O'Brien a bit off guard.

"What? A member?"

"Yeah. He's been a member for years. Jeez Sean, you of all people didn't know that?"

"A member of what?" asked O'Brien.

"Yeah. A member of what?" asked Mike as he turned to Weezer.

Weezer glanced at Mike and turned back to O'Brien.

"It's kinda like the help the poor club. We buy gifts for a needy family around Christmas. We leave the presents on the porch, ring the bell, and skedaddle. Nobody knows we were there. It's kinda like a Robin Hood thing. But that's what the club is all about. It's a secret. We don't want any publicity for what we do."

"Yeah, sure. What's the name of this club?" asked O'Brien.

"Why, it's called the..." Weezer looked about the room. "It's called the...Holy Cabinetry of the Brotherhood, I mean the Holy Brotherhood of the Cabinetry. Or as we like to call it, the HBC."

"I've never heard of such an organization," said O'Brien, "and I help teach the publics catechism on Sundays, you know."

"Sean, did you hear the man say it was a secret club?" said Mike, suddenly catching on. "There's a reason you've never heard of it. You're not a member."

"And Pope Paul is a member? Yeah, right," said O'Brien. "You guys are making this up because I caught you stealing from the church. Put it back or I'm going to tell Father Mallon."

Mike was inclined to agree with O'Brien and put the loot back, but Weezer pressed on. "I'd love to Sean, but we can't, even if we wanted to. It would violate the code. We can never violate the code. Never."

"What code is that?" asked O'Brien.

"The code of the HBC. That's about all I can say to a non-member. All I have to say is do you remember the Second Vatican Council? When they were allowed to say mass in English instead of Latin and all that other stuff? Do you remember?"

"Uh, yeah, sure. But I think I was in second grade."

"Well, I do, and let me tell you, it was groundbreaking. Not only do we say mass in English now, but did you hear the music that was played at mass today? Did you hear the guitars and the tambourine? Big difference from before, wouldn't you say?"

O'Brien had to agree. The music and words of the mass ritual certainly were different. "But what does that have to do with you stealing money from the church?"

"We're not stealing. The HBC was started during the Second Vatican Council. It was one of Pope Paul's personal projects. He only appointed a small number of members to start the HBC, but get this, their family members were also included, as long as they lived by the code. The purpose of the club is to do good deeds but be under the radar, like do-gooder ninjas, and that's what we were trying to do here."

"Have you ever read the Second Vatican Council, Sean?" continued Weezer.

"Uh, no."

"It's there, man.  The HBC is in there, but not too big.  Again, like I said, it's supposed to be a secret thing, but you seem like a good guy, Sean and you know your Catholic stuff.  Let me ask you this, would you like to be a member?"

O'Brien knitted his eyebrows and moved his head.  Weezer could tell that he had him on the edge between doubt and belief.  Mike stared at Weezer, in awe.

"Are you guys serious?  Is this on the level?  I mean, just who do you buy the presents for?"

"This year we're getting Christmas dinner and presents for the Fletchers.  Last year we helped the Lannigans."

O'Brien nodded his head.  He recalled that Mr. Lannigan suffered a heart attack and was laid up for over a year and still had seven children to feed.  It seemed to him that Weezer was involved in a very noble cause.

"You guys wait until Christmas?  What do you guys do with the money until then?"

"Well, we don't take much at one time," explained Weezer, "we don't want anyone getting suspicious, so we take a little at a time and then just save it up until then."

"Where do you keep it?"

"In a box, underneath Mike's back porch.  We both put anything we get into the box and bury it.  It adds up and then Mike and I go shopping around Christmas for the Fletchers, and believe you me, it sure makes us feel good.  Right Mike?"

Mike nodded and answered.  "Yep, it's the best feeling in the world.  Like a warm cup of hot chocolate going down on Christmas Eve."

"Come on Sean, help us out would ya?  The Fletchers sure could use the help. You know their story."

O'Brien did know the story.  The Fletchers lived about a block and a half away from him on Honore street.  Their story was tragic.  The Fletchers were not well off to begin with but when their toddler son died from pneumonia, the family was left with a mountain of doctor bills and other expenses.  O'Brien remembered his parents going to a fund raiser for them one night and then hearing the news the next day that an inebriated Mr. Fletcher was killed while driving home from the same event, leaving his wife and three grammar school-aged daughters behind.  He was sure that the family could use some assistance around that time of year.

"What would I have to do?"

"Well, normally we would just say see you in December for the shopping and delivery, but since this is your first time with us, we need to know that you're really in."

"I'm in.  I want to help the Fletchers."

Weezer made a solemn sign of the cross on O'Brien and then bowed his head.  Mike played along and bowed his head also, while keeping one eye on Weezer as to when he should raise his head.  Weezer raised his head and Mike followed along.

"Okay.  Here's the deal," said Weezer as he stepped closer to O'Brien.  He spoke in a low deliberate voice.

"Mike and I are going outside.  We will be waiting for you in the school hallway.  When you come out, you will hand us whatever you grab from the basket so we can add it to the box under Mike's porch."

O'Brien's face turned ashen.

"Sean, this is only your initiation to the HBC. This will be the only time you will do this.  From now on you will benefit from the joy and fun of spreading the happiness without having to do any of the dirty work.  Do you understand Sean?"  Weezer paused and stepped closer to O'Brien with the saddest eyes Sean had ever seen and whispered, "Remember the Fletchers.  They need us."

"You guys wait outside," said O'Brien.

Weezer and Mike obeyed, left the sacristy, and waited in the school hallway.

"What are we going to do come Christmas when he wants to leave gifts to the Fletchers?" said Mike.

"It won't matter. He's just as guilty as us now. He won't say a word about this to anybody."

Mike nodded in agreement when O'Brien emerged from the sacristy with a wad of envelopes and cash. He held them out to Weezer as if it were a handful of hot coals. Weezer quickly accepted them and stuffed them down his pants to be mingled with his own personal haul.

"Okay, let's get out of here."

Weezer and Mike ducked back into the church and headed for the front doors while O'Brien fled in another direction. Just as well, thought Weezer. He probably wouldn't see O'Brien over the summer, at least not until the school year started anyway.

The two altar boys exited the church through the huge dark glass front doors and gingerly walked down the steps for fear that their filthy lucre would slip out of their pants and expose them for the holy thieves that they were.

They walked south until they got to 71st Street, where they waited for traffic to allow them to safely cross the street. It would have to be a large gap in traffic, as neither boy wanted to have to run while concealing his stash.

"We got to find a place to pull this stuff out. It's starting to come down the leg of my pants," Mike said.

"Didn't you put them in your underpants?"

"No. Ugh, that's gross. You'll get dick cooties on the money."

Weezer shook his head in disbelief.

"Boy are you stupid. Everyone knows that you can't give yourself dick cooties. How else would you pee?"

Mike paused to think of what Weezer was saying.

"Hmm. Never thought of that."

"C'mon, we'll duck in the alley by Mrs. Murphy's garage."

They continued for another half block until they reached the entrance to the alley. Mike walked like he had a cast on his leg and started to lag behind Weezer, who's patience was running thin.

"C'mon, would ja?"

Mike tried to pick up the pace when a five-dollar bill slipped out from the bottom of his right pants leg.

"Hey, look at your pants," said Weezer as he pointed to Mike's pants. Mike looked down and realized he was leaking money like a rich scarecrow.

"Shit!" he said. Mike quickly tried to block its escape route, but his rapid movement caused more bills to slide out until he had a full-blown jail break of money sliding out from the bottom of his pants.

Dollar bills, fives and tens swirled in the wind as Mike desperately chased the fleeing greenbacks. Weezer could not help but laugh at the sight of Mike running down money like he was a contestant in some sort of urban game show.

Mike grabbed and saved what he could but missed some of the bills. The exhilaration of the heist was now tempered for him because of the lost money and probably more so by the way he lost it.

"C'mon, over here," waived Weezer standing next to a fifty-five-gallon garbage can. He reached into his pants and pulled out a wad of white envelopes and cash. His eyes widened as he surveyed his haul. He quickly sorted the cash by denomination and started counting.

"Fuckin' twenty-two dollars, man!"

Mike saw what Weezer held in his hand and his exhilaration reappeared. He reached into his pants and pulled out what he could, opened his pants, zipper down and let them drop to his ankles.

Numerous bills fell on to the ground as Mike stood there in his white Sears tidy-whitey underpants.

"Pull your pants up. I don't ever want to see that again!"

Weezer opened his first envelope and pulled out a check made payable to St. Justin for ten dollars.

"What the hell is this?" asked Weezer. "A check? What can I do with this?"

He turned to Mike, not expecting an answer. He didn't get one. Mike shrugged and counted his cash. Weezer opened another envelope. Another check for ten dollars to the church.

"Son of a..." cried Weezer.

"Nineteen bucks!" said Mike, not realizing the depth of Weezer's despair.

Weezer continued to open the envelopes that he had, and other than two fives in cash, the remainder were checks made out to the church. Weezer shook his head as he looked at the small pile of checks, about forty dollars' worth, that lay before him. He tore them in half, lifted the lid from the garbage can and threw them in. Mike followed suit but was not as disappointed. Other than when he made his Communion, he now possessed the largest amount of money he ever had in his life.

"So, what do you want to do?" said Weezer.

"The first thing I'm going to do is go to Strickey's. To hell with that penny candy, I'm getting a couple of nickel bars. And maybe even a Twinkie."

"That's cool. I could use a bag of chips and a pop."

The two boys walked down the alley in the direction of the store.

"So, you want to go to the movies?" said Weezer.

"I dunno. I already saw "Patton" and there's nothing else that I want to see. Are the Sox home?" said Mike, knowing that Weezer as the resident Sox fan would know.

"No. They're in Baltimore. I know, let's go bowling."

"Yeah, cool. Alright," said Mike. "We need the practice. The summer league starts soon. Did you check with your parents yet about joining?"

"Naw. Ain't no big deal. My dad's a big bowler. He bowls three nights a week. I'm joining. We still need a fourth. Bullethead said he would be on our team. He's even getting a new ball for the season."

"Ooh. That's a good idea. Get some shoes too, save money over the long run," replied Mike.

Soon the boys were sitting on the sidewalk in front of the neighborhood candy store, each sipping on a cold bottle of Pepsi. Weezer ate from a bag of chips while Mike worked on a package of Twinkies, then started on a Hershey Bar with Almonds. He chewed the sweet chocolate as it formed on the corners of his mouth. Weezer looked at him in disgust.

"Wipe your lips, will you? You look like you're taking a crap through your mouth."

Being the fourteen-year-old smart-ass that he was, Mike slowly pushed the dark brown candy bar through his lips which caused Weezer more distress.

"Oh, man. You are a sick puppy."

Mike smiled and sucked the brown chocolate back into his mouth. He took another bite from the Hershey bar and combined it with the mass of chocolate already in his mouth, enjoying it and the warm sun.

It wasn't hot, it was nice, thought Weezer as he pulled on his bottle of Pepsi. The leaves of the trees waved in the breeze while the distant sound of a lawn mower accompanied them in their arboreal ballet. Sparrows flew through the trees, chirping in a common dialect that only they could decipher, yet Weezer sensed a rhythm in their sounds and tried to follow along. He knew they were communicating between each other. He just knew it.

Mike let out a loud belch.

"Good one," said Weezer.

Just then, Mr. Bukevich, the store owner, emerged from the front door of the store, wearing a white apron and smoking a Lucky Strike.

"Okay, you guys. Go. Shoo. Go away. This isn't a hangout," he told them.

Weezer and Mike stood up, and slowly walked away.

"So, bowling?" said Weezer.

"Yeah, let's go," answered Mike as he took a long final drink from his Pepsi. He let out another loud belch and tossed the empty bottle on the front lawn of a house as they passed.

"You're not going to save that bottle for the deposit? Oh, that's right, you're Mr. Moneybags now," said Weezer.

"Hell yeah, I am. This money is burning a hole in my pocket. Let's take the train to the bowling alley. We'll get there quicker."

The half-mile walk to the tracks took them west on 72nd Street. They walked in silence for the first couple of blocks as they took in the smells, sounds and general vibes of a beautiful Sunday afternoon. The act that would direct them straight to hell at the Pearly Gates was far from their mind.

Weezer liked the sounds of summer: the distant lawn mowers, the omnipresent traffic and construction, birds chirping. He appreciated the radio blasting from the open window of a passing car, the lazy and systematic tossing of water on the sidewalk by the newfangled sprinklers that went back and forth instead of round and round, and the whirring of the electric box fan in the window of his bedroom. The summer sounds were brighter and louder than winter sounds, which are muted and gray. The car tire spinning in the street or the shovel on the sidewalk after a snowfall, these were muffled sounds that emanated from a miserable situation.

Summer sounds were different.  There was a hope in the sounds of early summer.  This was the best part of the summer, thought Weezer.  It was not yet crazy hot nor were there any mosquitos and then there were the sounds, which were new again, as they were every year when they arrived at this time.

The light breeze jostled the trees just enough so that you knew they were there.  The neighborhood had been developed long ago and the trees in the area were large and prominent.  In the fall, when the mammoth trees shed their leaves, Weezer, under orders from his father, raked them into a pile at the street curb.  Then Weezer's father would come out with a couple of potatoes.  He would bury them into the leaf pile, light a Camel and then the leaves.  After much huffing and blowing from Weezer's father, the leaves would ignite and the orange flames that shot up at the beginning of the burn would soon dissolve into smoldering red embers that acted as a primitive urban convection oven in which the hard and raw potatoes would turn into a delicious fall treat for Weezer and his father.

There was something about the taste of a potato that came from a burning leaf pile.  After an hour or so, the skin would turn into a black crust that would be cracked open like the enchanted egg of some fire-breathing creature.  Steam would rise from the open gash revealing the delicious white meat of the potato.

Weezer's dad smuggled butter, salt, and a fork for each of them. He looked back at the house before he handed Weezer a fork.

"Your mother would kill me if she saw that I brought these out of the house.  It'll be our little secret, okay?"

Weezer smiled and enthusiastically nodded as he took the fork. Together they sat on the curb and placed their still steaming hot potato on the curb next to them.  They took turns slathering hunks of butter and showers of salt on the potato and then started to dig in.

Weezer ate the first bite, and the butter, salt and bits of charred potato skin turned it into the best thing he had ever eaten.  It was a hot treat on a warm night, but it didn't matter to Weezer. He liked the warmth. He looked up at his father who was also in the middle of his first bite.

"Hmm," he savored the first taste of the potato. He looked down at Weezer and smiled. He took another forkful of potato and put it into his mouth. As he ate the potato, he stared straight ahead. Then he started to cry.

* * * * * * *

"Beautiful day," said Mike.

"Yeah. I can't wait until fall," said Weezer, still in the haze of thoughts about his father.

"Fall? We just got out of school this week," said Mike.

"I mean for bowling. The fall leagues," said Weezer meekly.

"Are you joining the fall league?" asked Mike.

"I think so. I'm digging this bowling stuff. What about you?"

"I don't know. Saturday mornings has some pretty good TV on."

"You still watch cartoons? You little baby."

"No, I don't watch cartoons. There are other things on other than cartoons, you know," said Mike.

"Like what?"

"HR Pufnstuf and the Banana Splits. I watch those. Neither of those are cartoons."

"You'd rather watch those shows than bowl? How old are you again?"

"Same age as you, dickhead. I just like those shows, that's all."

Weezer shook his head in mock disgust.

"Alright, alright. But you're still a little pussy."

They arrived at the end of the line where the right-of-way for the railroad began, which was marked by a cyclone fence to prevent trespassers. The fence was rusted and bent over almost parallel to the ground where the sidewalk ended.  All one had to do was to walk over the dead fence and have access to the rails and their deadly convenience.

Which is what Weezer and Mike did.

The railroad tracks were about fifty yards or so from where the sidewalk ended.  The four sets of tracks ran north-south from God knows where to God knows where.  They would hop the freight train at 72nd Street and take it for a half mile and after a wide right turn at an intersection, to the 75th Street viaduct on Western Avenue, where they would let go of the box car ladder and tumble to the embankment before the train built up speed for the oncoming straightaway.

There were certain rules one had to follow when flipping a train.  Familiarity with the stretch of tracks where your target train would run is key.  The speed of the train down this stretch would tell Weezer and Mike whether it was the right train for them.  The train they wanted would be taking a wide right turn to Western and approached the intersection at a slower speed than the trains that were going straight.

You also need a destination.  One does not just hop on the trains for fun as that would be downright dangerous.  You need to know when and where the trains would be slowing down for your dismount.  Weezer had heard stories of two guys from a neighboring parish, Little Flower, that had hopped a train just for fun, not knowing where it was going.  The train sped up on a straightaway and never slowed down enough for the two to hop off.  They had to call their parents from Kansas or somewhere to come pick them up.

Both Weezer and Mike were experienced at using the local railroad for commuting purposes. It got you to where you wanted to go, and a long walk could be turned into a thrilling adventure.  Of course, they had heard stories of other kids losing various appendages while doing the same thing, usually from a third-hand source, but without names or specific circumstances of the appendage losers, the stories morphed into neighborhood legends, like the two idiots who could not get off the train until Kansas.

Weezer and Mike appreciated the dangers and the risk involved in their chosen mode of transportation. Mike, for one, would not look down at the steel train wheels that were rotating on the track about six inches from his front toe, instead he would look down over the terrain that they passed. The backyards of houses, a little league baseball field and the eighteenth hole of Windy Hills Golf Club. The railroad was supposed to be partitioned from the locations of civilized leisure by a small line of trees that ran parallel to the tracks, but the trees did not grow as originally planned. Instead, they evolved into a grotesque gnarl of half bush-half tree that grew horizontally and formed a continuous mangled barrier between the railroad tracks and the area's playgrounds.

Weezer, on the other hand, appreciated the exhilaration of the entire situation. He not only looked at the train wheels next to his feet but would touch the rolling wheel with the tip of his gym shoe for a quick second. Once before he held it there for too long and the wheel cut into the toe of his shoe, which was tough to explain when he got home but well worth the rush. In addition, he would take one foot off the ladder and hold on with one hand while the train made a wide right turn, hanging from the box car like a big human X. The inertia from the turn would threaten to pull him from the train and down the rocky embankment into an area of large concrete slab remnants.

Once the turn was completed, the train would start to speed up for the oncoming straight-away. That was Weezer and Mike's cue to bail and try to softly tumble down the embankment to a gap between the viaduct and the warehouse that fronted Western Avenue, where they slid down to the sidewalk and walked the remaining half-block to Woodmac Bowl.

It was open bowling that Sunday afternoon.  The lanes were barely half full as Weezer and Mike walked into the air-conditioned comfort of the 16-lane establishment.  It had a small burger stand, a bar and a pro shop. Weezer stared into the window that displayed shoes, shirts, gloves, balls, and bags.

"I'm getting a ball," Weezer declared.

"Hmm, okay," Mike replied.

Together they walked into the shop and went to the glass counter where the proprietor, or more probably, the son of the proprietor, was reading the Sunday Sun-Times he had laid out on the counter.  He wore a bowling shirt with the name "Chip" embroidered over the left breast pocket.  He looked up from the paper.

"Can I help you guys?"

"Yeah," Weezer said.  "I want to buy a bowling ball.  How much are they?"

"Oh, they range anywhere from Twenty-Five dollars to a hundred and fifty or more."

"Twenty-five, huh?" said Weezer.  He reached into his pocket and pulled out the remaining cash he had on hand and counted it. He had exactly twenty-five dollars.  He would need money for the tax.  He turned to Mike.

"I need a couple of bucks for the taxes.  Can you help me out?"

"Yeah, sure.  I guess."

"Thanks, man."

Weezer turned back to the counter.

"Okay, what do you have for twenty-five bucks."

Chip turned to the boxed bowling balls that lay on the shelves behind him and took stock of what he could do for Weezer. He felt sympathetic to the boy's plight.  It was not too many years ago when he himself would save the money from working part-time for his father to purchase his bowling gear.  Of course, he may have had a different attitude towards his young customer if he knew that the source of Weezer's funds was courtesy of the attendees of St. Justin's 12:30 Mass.

He came back to the counter with a scruffy bowling ball box and laid it on the counter. He flipped open the top and pulled out a pre-drilled black AMF Three Dot ball and showed it to Weezer.

"This ball was returned to us. See here, it's a replug," Chip said as he pointed to 3 circles on the ball. "The holes were re-filled with resin, allowed to set, and it's as good as brand new. There wasn't even a name on the ball yet. It's never been used."

"So why was it returned?" said Weezer.

"I don't know. It was bought for one of these kids who hop the trains to get around and, well, he lost his fingers somehow on the train and I guess he can't bowl anymore. At least that's what I heard."

Weezer glanced at Mike's terrified face.

Chip sensed the hesitation and sweetened the pot.

"I'll even stamp your name on the ball. Up to five letters."

"I'll take it!" said Weezer.

And the fitting began. Chip took the necessary measurements from Weezer's right hand, applied them to the shiny black orb with drills and brushes and brought the ball back for Weezer's approval.

He placed Weezer's middle two fingers and thumb into the freshly drilled holes and let the ball slip and drop from Weezer's hand onto a specially constructed pad on the counter.

"How's that feel?"

"Fine." Weezer held the ball by himself and swung it back and forth.

"I like it," said Weezer.

"It's sixteen pounds. It may seem a little heavy now, but you'll grow into it."

Weezer nodded in agreement.

"Now what name do you want stamped on the ball? Up to five letters."

"Weezer," said Weezer.

"That's six. Only five. The machine can only do five at the most. You want 'Weeze'?"

Mike snickered.

"No. That doesn't really sound right," said Weezer.

"Okay. What about your initials? What's your name?"

"Gary O'Donnell."

"Perfect. I'll even throw in the apostrophe for free."

Chip imprinted Weezer's initials-G. O'D on the ball behind the counter and returned it to him. The ball was repackaged within its used cardboard box.

"Well, let's get some lanes," Weezer said as they walked up to the main counter. "I can't wait to use this ball."

"You guys need shoes?" said the employee at the counter as he assigned them lane 6.

"Yeah," said both boys in unison.

After getting their sizes, the employee retrieved the proper shoes and placed them on the counter.

"Half a buck each," he said.

Mike reached into his pocket, pulled out a dollar and placed it on the counter. "Here's for me," he said.

"I ain't got any money," Weezer said to Mike as if he should have known.

Mike shook his head, "That will be for the both of us."

"Does this mean I have to pay for the bowling too? What the hell man," said Mike as he realized that the rest of the afternoon would have to be on him.

"Just a couple of games. I have to try out this ball. Oh, and maybe a pop and a bag of pretzels. That's it. I'll pay you back."

"Yeah, right. C'mon," Mike said as he made his attitude known by storming away from the counter towards their assigned lane. Weezer snickered as he followed Mike.

After they changed their shoes, Weezer started to fill out the score sheet while Mike went for two pops and two bags of pretzels and to find a house ball that fit him.

While Mike roamed about the racks of balls that lined the main aisle of the establishment looking for the perfect fit, Weezer took his new ball from the box and wiped it with his tee shirt. The ball reflected a glossy black image that heightened the three white dots on the ball and the white lettering of the AMF logo. Above the logo were Weezer's initials, also in white, but a brighter white from the still fresh putty. He smiled as he looked at his reflection in the virgin ball.

It will never be this shiny again, thought Weezer. After the first roll down the lane, the scuffs and smudges will start to appear. Sure, you can have the ball buffed in that noisy machine next to the bar window, and it will come out all shiny and clean, but it wouldn't be new shiny. Not like the ball was now.

He wished his father could see his ball while it was new. His Dad would appreciate the value of getting a used ball that was customed to fit Weezer's hand. His father would also appreciate it when Weezer would tell him that he had saved money from his paper route to buy the ball.

Mike came back to the alley with a ball that he had found and placed it on the return rack.

"Be right back," Mike said. "Gonna get the pop and pretzels."

The lights above the set pins at the end of the alley were lit which indicated that the lanes were ready to bowl on. Weezer stepped up on the lane with his new shiny ball and prepared to take a practice shot. In one of his rare pointers to Weezer, his father had stressed the importance of the practice shot as an indicator as to how oily the lane was.  The more oil, the more hook on the shot.

Keeping his father's advice in mind, Weezer rolled his ball down the lane with a medium twist of his wrist, which caused the ball to hook into the far gutter.

Mike arrived with the pop and pretzels in time to watch the virgin roll of Weezer's new ball.

"You suck," he said.

"Do you wanna make a bet on the game?  I'll give you ten pins and we'll bet for the money I owe you.  How's that?"

Realizing that he should not have run his mouth, Mike meekly said, "No.  Not today."

"I thought so," said Weezer as he retrieved his ball from the return rack.

He placed three fingers into the ball and held it before him.  There was a scuff on the ball from his first roll.  He let out a sigh and lined up for his second shot.  This time he would use a little less twist in his wrist.  He rolled the ball down the lane and hit the pocket squarely, knocking down all ten pins.

"Okay, I got this," he said as he took a seat at the scorer's table.

Mike was not the bowler that Weezer was.  Mike tended to throw the ball in a straight line as hard as he could.  More often than not, despite his velocity, he would be left with two or three pins still standing after the first shot.  Weezer would shake his head at Mike's technique, having given up long ago on trying to teach him anything about the game.  Mike was a thrower, thought Weezer, not a bowler.

The three games went well for Weezer.  It took but three or four frames to get used to the new ball and after that, he bowled the best that he could recall for the remaining frames.  He was beaming at the results of the day.  He sat at the scorer's table and did some quick math with the scores from the three games. Mike was changing his shoes.

"Man, a 452 series. I can't remember when I did better. It would have been even better if not for the first couple of frames."

"I broke a hundred," said Mike as he laced up his shoes.

"You don't listen. You just throw the ball."

"Well, doesn't everybody throw the ball?"

"Never mind," said Weezer as he packed his ball into the cardboard box. "Next week, I'll get me a bag and some shoes. After that, I may even go out bowling with my old man."

"He's pretty serious. You got game for that?"

"I do now," Weezer said as he held up the box by the makeshift handle that was cut into the sides of the box.

Having returned their shoes to the counter and Mike paying for the bowling, the two boys headed home via the same route, but in reverse. After climbing up the viaduct via the gap in the wall, they would flip the train as it slowed into the wide turn and headed north to where they would hop off at 72nd Street.

Weezer held the bowling ball box with his right hand as he grasped the rail boxcar ladder of the slow-moving train with his left. Mike flipped the boxcar behind Weezer and grasped firmly with both hands to the ladder, being careful not to look down at the steel wheels inches from his toes. Instead, he looked straight ahead at Weezer, dangling from the ladder with his left hand while holding the boxed bowling ball with his right hand.

The train approached the wide turn and Weezer once again used the inertia of the turn to hang off the boxcar by one hand and one foot, only this time the added weight of the ball in the box caused him to grip the ladder rung tighter and wonder to himself if this was not a good idea.

Suddenly, in mid-turn, the handle on the ragged cardboard box snapped. The shiny bowling ball fell on the concrete slabs at the bottom of the embankment, where it bounced high and over the low trees that separated the tracks from the golf course.

Weezer watched in horror as his shiny new bowling ball bounced away from him and down the embankment.  He could only watch as the ball disappeared.

He looked at Mike on the boxcar behind him who, while firmly grasping the rung, was laughing at Weezer's dilemma.

Weezer turned away as a small tear rolled down his cheek.

# WINDY HILLS G.C.
# June 1970

Father Tom Mallon sat before the small desk in his room holding a glass of scotch, neat. The indirect glow from the streetlights outside the open windows and the desk lamp were all the light he needed. He stared at the empty wicker collection basket that lay at his feet and then turned to the neatly stacked bills and checks that lay on the desk directly beneath the lamp. He finished the scotch and replenished it from the bottle that was also on the desk, but in the shadows, away from the light.

He was playing the human card with himself again, that he was susceptible to sin, to vice, to bad habits, to the same human qualities that he was put on earth to tame in others. He loved to pull out the card for some of his behavior at times, like the second scotch he had just poured, but where was the line? The point of no-return. The abyss where one bad step, one bad move can send you plummeting into...into what? The drinking was an occupational hazard. Hell, it was probably the only job in the world where you must drink to do your job properly. Every morning at mass. Sommeliers at least get to spit the wine out. We can't do that as spitting out the blood of Christ would certainly give a bad impression to the congregants. We must drink every day to properly do our jobs. And not only that, but it's also mostly done in the morning, for Christ sakes!

He smiled at his unintentional literalism. And then he lost control of his mind and thoughts of why, dipped in hindsight, took over.

The weave of his life with that of Freddy Gallagher and Uncle Wally had unraveled and broken apart like a once taut rope that had become frayed from time and the elements. The individual strands slowly frazzled and retreated until a snap from the survivor completes the total and violent final separation.

He felt an enormous sense of relief, like someone had lifted a small Buick from his chest. But he also felt a sadness. A sadness from retrospection. Of what could have been.

After Catherine died, Tommy went to live with Uncle Wally in the upstairs apartment of a three-flat on 71st Street, just off Paulina. It was only two blocks from where Catherine had her apartment, so Tommy did not have to make a whole new batch of friends and stayed enrolled in St. Justin as if nothing happened. Additionally, it moved him closer to Freddy's house, which further solidified their friendship.

Freddy had never met Tommy's father, but he did meet Catherine a couple of times. Years later, when they both worked for Uncle Wally, Freddy would confide to Tommy that Catherine gave him the creeps. Instead of punching him in the face, Tommy simply said, "Yeah. I get it."

For whatever reason, Wally did not get along with Freddy. Tommy sensed an awkward vibe between the two, with most of the awkwardness coming from Wally. In contrast, he felt that Freddy looked up to Uncle Wally as some sort of mentor, or at least a connection with a world he wished to be involved with.

Tommy appreciated Uncle Wally's attempts at parenthood but also understood that they would not last. At first, Wally tried to be at home every night to make dinner for him and Tommy, but that faded after about a week as Wally's various business dealings called for him to spend some late afternoons in the local gin mills. He called it "bill collecting," which Tommy did not understand, but accepted. He didn't mind making his own dinner anyway. Some nights it would be soup and sandwich, usually peanut butter, other nights a bowl of Special K. Once he attempted a tuna casserole after he found the recipe in an old cookbook of Catherine's. He told Uncle Wally that he had saved the leftovers for him, but they both forgot and a couple of weeks later Tommy came across what looked like a science experiment in the fridge and threw it out.

After a while, Tommy would accompany Uncle Wally as he made his "bill collecting" rounds. While Uncle Wally conducted business, Tommy would scale onto a bar stool where he would order either a hard-boiled egg or a bag of potato chips. Some nights he would order both. While Tommy sat at the bar eating his supper, Uncle Wally would be collecting on his "bills." It was usually a different tavern each time, but on the way home Uncle Wally would stop by Big Eddie Sloan's house. He would pull his shiny black 1947 Studebaker Commander, the love of his life, in front of Big Eddie's large home, tell Tommy to wait, and with the car still running, get out and run up the stairs of the home and drop an envelope in a slot in the front door.

"The bosses cut. Got to do it," he would always say. Tommy would nod as if he knew what Uncle Wally was talking about and forget it. Eventually he would understand what it was, and Uncle Wally would let him make the drop at Sloan's house while he waited behind the wheel of the Studebaker.

Uncle Wally was a street philosopher who prided himself on being able to quickly tell what kind of man he was speaking to after just meeting him.  He believed that he had deep insights into one's soul after conversing for a few moments, but sometimes his own bias would cloud or slant these insights.  As an example, if he learned that you were a Cubs fan, he would be troubled for your spiritual future as it was obvious that you did not know your ass from a hole in the ground and you would be doomed to a life of bad decisions and their results.

Uncle Wally taught Tommy and Freddy how to rationalize the dark side of man. He told the boys that God intentionally made man to be imperfect, so God does not expect much from man, maybe attend a mass now and then. So, a certain amount of vice should be expected from an imperfect man.  Vice makes God an existential carrot on a stick that man will never reach, never attain, but it gives man something to strive for, to exist.  Uncle Wally felt that he was acting as a spiritual social worker by encouraging vice, his specialty being gambling, whose main purpose was to keep God relevant to man.

"I'm doing God's will" Uncle Wally would say.  Catherine would admonish him for his heresy, and Richard would roll his eyes but neither contested Uncle Wally's beliefs, so Tommy just let them be at that.

Father Mallon's mind delved farther with each drink of the scotch he was sipping.  The dusty layers of his recall were each stripped away and revealed a new layer beneath it, as if it were brand new.  Hindsight will do that.  Turn a fuzzy movie into focus so it can be seen better, and maybe, just maybe, be learned from.

He recalled when Freddy entered the big picture.  Uncle Wally was adamant about his feelings toward Freddy.  "That kid ain't right," he would say. "In fact, he's just plain evil.  I want no part of him."

Despite Uncle Wally's aversion to him, Freddy came around often to visit Tommy.  Tommy sensed Uncle Wally's dislike of Freddy but did not really care.  He could not understand why, as Freddy was a great friend and knew quite a bit about the streets, probably more than Tommy.  Business was picking up and they could use a little help collecting from the easy accounts, so he could not grasp what the animosity was about on Uncle Wally's part.  He never talked with either of the parties about his sense, so now it seemed like so much water under the bridge.

But the relationship between Uncle Wally and Freddy seemed to change on Tommy's 16th birthday.  Or at least thaw a little bit.

Wally told Tommy to invite his friends over to the apartment for his birthday and he would bring home a birthday cake.  Tommy was genuinely excited but being sixteen meant that he could not show it.

"I'll just have Freddy come over for some cake," he said.

That evening Wally fulfilled his promise and brought home a Dressel's Bakery whipped-cream cake with shaved bits of chocolate on top.

"Got candles too," said Wally as he placed the boxed cake on the kitchen table.  Tommy opened the box and pulled the cake out, being careful not to leave any of the valuable whipped-cream frosting on the inside of the box.

Wally returned with candles in hand.  "Sorry, Tommy.  They only came in packs of ten," explained Wally as he put the tenth and last candle into the top of the cake.  He lit a match, lit the first candle, then used the candle to light the remaining nine on the cake.  When he was finished, he started the birthday song.

"Happy birthday to you…" sang Wally.

Freddy joined along.

"Happy birthday to you, happy birthday dear Tommy, happy birthday to you."

Tommy blew out the candles and enjoyed the whiff of the melting wax that rose from the extinguished candles.

Father Mallon still distinctly remembered the aroma of the candles from that day.  He rose from his chair and went to his closet and looked on the top shelf.  He pulled out a shoe box, reached in and took out a sheathed six-inch knife with an intricately carved handle of a reindeer figure standing in front of a large tree.

He sat back down and pulled the knife from the sheath and closely examined the blade.  This could certainly do some damage to a person, he thought.  Or cut cake.

With the aroma of wax still hanging in the air, Freddy laid his birthday present on the table.

"Hold it, Uncle Wally.  Let Tommy open his gift first.  It'll come in handy."

"Aw, look at that," said Wally.  "Freddy brought you a present."

"You didn't have to do that," said Tommy.

"It's no big deal," said Freddy.  "I found it."

Freddy handed the present, which was wrapped in the Sunday Comics section of the Chicago Tribune, to Tommy and said, "Happy birthday."

Tommy tore off the paper, which revealed a beautifully decorated knife enclosed in an elaborately beaded leather sheath.  He pulled the knife out and looked at the shiny blade in awe.

"Wow," said Tommy, while still staring at the magnificent blade. "Thank you."

Wally had turned ashen white when he saw what Tommy had unwrapped.

"This is cool," said Tommy. "Where did you get this?"

Freddy turned to Wally and said, "Over at Bubbly Creek.  I think it was Halloween."

The blood continued to drain from Wally's face as Freddy smiled at him watching Tommy cut the cake with the knife.

The next week, despite what he had stated earlier, Uncle Wally ordained Freddy as part of the crew.

Father Mallon remembered the look on Uncle Wally's face. There was something between them that he was in the dark about.

Wally also taught Tommy and Freddy the ins and outs of dealing poker. And taking bets on horses. And policy. And dice games. And various other forms of taking a workingman's honest wages with a smile. The smile was the key. Most gamblers know that it was their fault for making a losing wager, and if Uncle Wally could ease the pain a bit with a smile while taking their money from them it would be less painful. Or so Uncle Wally thought. Well after Tommy became Father Mallon and while Freddy was doing time for fencing marijuana and snow tires, Uncle Wally leaned over a table at Nicky's Tavern, with a smile, to collect from Al Smith, one of his "bills," when he accidently knocked over a drink on Al's wife. Al, known as Smitty by everyone who knew him, was a sore loser and a jealous man.

"You think this is funny?" said Al.

"Why no, Smitty. I'm sorry. Real sorry," Wally said apologetically.

"You smilin' mother fucker!" said Al.

Smitty broke his beer bottle on the edge of the table and ran it hard into Wally's chest. Smitty and his party left the tavern through the back door as Wally lay in an expanding pool of his blood on the floor. When the police arrived, no one admitted seeing anything.

Years later Father Mallon found out who killed Uncle Wally when hearing a confession at St. Justin. An aged voice from behind the confessional screen confessed to him that he was present in Nicky's during that day and that he had witnessed Smitty's transgression but did not say anything to the cops. He asked for Father Mallon's absolution. He gave it, but he added an additional ten Hail Marys on his penance. It was the least he could do for Uncle Wally, he thought.

Father Mallon poured himself another drink and mumbled, "to Uncle Wally." He took a long sip and turned to the stacks of money and checks on the desk.  He was thankful that it was still there and not in Freddy Gallagher's pocket like it was the last time the two golfed together.

He then turned to the heavy object laying on his bed, covered with a golf towel.  After a hard and slow gaze, he finished his drink.

There was a knock on his door.  He walked to the door, opened it, and said, "Come in."

Father Burke, dressed in priest casual, which was the top button of his black shirt open, and the white collar removed, entered the room.

"Hey Father Mallon.  How are you?"

"I'm good Billy, how about you?"  Father Mallon used William Burke's real first name.  He had a personal rule that if you are dressed priest casual and are alone, he would address you by your given birth name.

"Fine, fine.  I'm going to bed now and I was hoping to make the bank deposit tomorrow morning.  Will the offerings be ready?"

"Yeah, no problem, Billy."  Father Mallon indicated the stacks of money and checks on his desk.

"I just have to make out the deposit slips.  I'm a little behind things after what happened today."

"I understand," said Father Burke.  "Is there anything I can do?  It must have been traumatic."

"Yeah, it was pretty bloody, but I'm good.  A couple of cocktails, some prayer and a good night's sleep and I'll be ready to go."

Father Burke had no response, just a nervous question.  "So, will, can, is, the deposit ready?"

Father Mallon smiled and sat back in his chair.  "I'll slip it under your door before I go to bed."

"Thank you, Father Mallon.  I hope that with the Lord's help, you will deal with this unfortunate and very, very, nasty, event."

"Thank you, Billy.  Now go to bed."

Father Burke backed out of the room and closed the door behind him. Father Mallon reached back into the shadows for the bottle of scotch, poured himself another and sat back in his chair.

He knew he was flippant with Billy, but he didn't feel good about it. He certainly did not feel that way, but the casual way that he dismissed the entire episode while talking with Billy made him feel as if he was in some sort of act of denial. That what happened today, didn't happen.

He thought long about his first round of golf with Freddy. He remembered it well. It was a beautiful spring morning that even a bad golf day couldn't ruin. But a bad golf day with Freddy Gallagher could.   The unfortunate part of Mallon's bad golf day was that he did not realize it was a bad golf day until he and Freddy approached the 18th hole and he asked Freddy what the scores were. Freddy stopped, grabbed the scorecard from his pull cart, and totaled up the back nine holes. He looked up at Mallon and said, "You owe me two hundred dollars."

The beautiful day turned into the tornado from the Wizard of Oz for Mallon.

"What?"

"I've parred every hole so far. Two hundred dollars chief."

He handed the scorecard to Mallon who quickly totaled up the numbers and came up with the same result.

He did make the bet. That he knew. Why was another matter. He had long held his habit of placing personal funds in jeopardy on the outcome of meaningless events in check since his arrival at St. Justin. However, the word, 'Sure' slid from his tongue and out into the open air like a dark wispy cloud of déjà vu in response to Freddy's proposal on the first tee.

He also realized that Freddy was serious about collecting on the bet. Freddy called him "chief," which Mallon recognized from the 'good old days' of Uncle Wally. To Freddy, this was strictly business, a day at the office.  He had made some incredible shots during the round, none of which Mallon saw, but he believed that he made them on the square.  Freddy wouldn't hustle a priest, especially a priest who was a life-long friend.

Or would he?

Mallon had thoughts of cancelling the second outing, but he had no tangible proof that Freddy had hustled him, and he also felt a strange and primal testosteronal urge to be made whole again.  A lay person would call it payback.

It was, however, the conversation that he had with Father Cummins at the ballgame that convinced him that he should encourage Freddy to start his own Lost Boys Club.  The concept of focusing on an individual with spiritual potential was interesting to him and he believed that Freddy certainly had potential.  If only he could prevent him from taking a ball-peen hammer to his kneecap during the process.

Mallon had convinced himself that his act of paying the golf debt to Freddy with church collections was for the benefit of the parish in that a priest without a broken arm would be better for the congregation than a priest with a broken arm.  He knew it was a weak and cowardly rationalization and it was also the source of the underlying desperation that hung about him like humidity on a hot day in August.

The future of his vocation was at stake today.  He could not afford to lose to Freddy again, especially for the stakes that he had lost the last time, but he felt now that he knew what he was up against.  He would keep an eye on Freddy's every shot, he would keep his own scorecard, and he would shoot the round that he is capable of shooting.  He had been out at the range three times this week in anticipation for this event and he felt good.

A wiser and more confident Father Mallon drove his aqua blue Ford Torino into the parking lot of the Wind Hills Golf Club and pulled into the first empty parking space. It was just off the raised green of the 18th hole. He got out of his car, opened the trunk hood, and sat on the lip of the trunk to change into his golf shoes. It was a beautiful day, sunny and warm with a gentle breeze. It would be a good day to walk the course. Save a couple of bucks and get some exercise. Wealth and Health. He suddenly had an idea for the next week's homily. He took out a small notebook that he constantly carried with him and jotted down his idea. The golf game has paid off already.

He started to pull his clubs out when a dark green 1968 Mustang pulled into the parking lot and honked. Mallon smiled and waved at Freddy.

"Tommy, Tommy, Tommy! It's good to see you again!" said an excited Freddy as he approached Mallon with open arms.

A cautious Mallon accepted the obligatory hug. Freddy took a step back and looked at him up and down.

"Looking good, buddy. Hey, let me get my shoes and clubs. Come on over, take a look at my new ride," Freddy said.

They approached a freshly washed and waxed Ford Mustang. A thing of beauty for any beholder.

"This is the same car that Steve McQueen drove in Bullitt. Well, not the same car, but the same model. 1968 Mustang. Fastback."

"This is amazing Freddy," said Mallon as he shook his head and walked towards the car. He ran his hand over the front hood and said "wow."

"Three hundred ninety cubic inches of bad boy under that hood. Over three hundred twenty horsepower. When I get on the highway, it just makes me want to jack-off."

"I'll take your word on that. Freddy this car is beautiful, just gorgeous."

"Feel like walking today?" asked Mallon. "Seems like a nice day."

"Sure, sure. Stretch the legs out. I get it," Freddy said. "How's the game been lately?"

"Could always be better. I've been trying some new clubs out."

"Good. I feel the same. Shall we make it interesting? I'll give you a chance to get your money back."

"Sure," said Mallon.

After checking in, they walked to the first tee. Mallon approached it with trepidation rooted in a sense that he was experiencing the grown-up version of Freddy. This Freddy was the root cause of his relapse to wagering more than he could afford on stupid bets. This Freddy had less joy and more malicious underpinnings. This Freddy did not have his back.

The conversation with Father Cummins kept roiling in his mind as he was developing a genuine concern for Freddy's spiritual well-being. He had never looked at Freddy in the spiritual sense before, but now he sensed a possibility of reaching out to him and making a connection. As a priest, he felt that he was an expert of the soul, especially someone else's. He felt that his genuine spiritual concern for Freddy confirmed his life choice, his calling and what he was meant to do.

Also, Freddy took his money the last time out. Getting even is not revenge.

Mallon teed up his ball on the first hole. A long par five. He swung hard and hooked it.

"Shit!" yelled Mallon.

"Hey, hey, hey, man. You're a priest. You can't talk like that anymore. What the fuck," said Freddy.

"Sorry," said Mallon. "This game can bring out the worse in me sometimes."

"I'll say," said Freddy as he approached the tee. He lined up his shot and drove it almost two hundred fifty yards down the middle of the fairway.

They walked together for about one-hundred and fifty yards as Freddy formulated his proposal.

"So, what say?  Same terms as last time?" asked Freddy.

Mallon pretended that he did not hear him.  Freddy repeated his question.

"Hey Padre.  Do you want to make up for last time?"

"That's a little steep for me," Mallon replied.

"Alright, alright.  I was just giving you an opportunity to win the church's money back, that's all.  You know, like a bake sale," said Freddy.

"I told you I paid that back," said Mallon despite his not paying it back.  "Okay, same as last time."

They walked in silence for another fifty yards and then separated, Freddy walking straight ahead and Mallon veering to the left to find his ball in the rough.

Mallon kicked the tall grass where he thought his ball went but failed to find it.  He turned and looked at Freddy strolling down the fairway with his back turned to him.  He could not let Freddy get out of sight, so he reached into his pants pocket, pulled out a second ball and softly rolled it out on the fairway leaving him with a pretty good lie about 140 yards from the hole.  He would have to take the penalty.

Mallon addressed his new ball, took a perfect swing, and lofted his ball into the air.  With his club still over his left shoulder from his follow through, he watched his shot as it just missed Freddy's head by about two inches and landed ten yards from the green.  Freddy turned around with outstretched arms and yelled, "What the fuck, Padre?"

"Sorry," Mallon yelled back.

He turned to his golf bag and muttered: "Just letting you know I'm watching," and returned his seven-iron into the bag.

The next three holes occurred without any suspicion on Mallon's part, as both parties stayed on the fairways and within eyesight of each other. Keeping his own scorecard, Mallon tallied a slight lead for Freddy, due to his disastrous first hole.

On the fifth hole, after the tee shots, Freddy and Mallon were neck and neck on the rising fairway that peaked about halfway to the hole and hid a water hazard that lay just out of sight.

Mallon shot first lofting his ball high and to the left over the crest in the fairway. It was a blind shot, but he assumed it was a good shot as he hit it where he was aiming.

Freddy shot next, and he also lofted his ball over the crest, but to the left of where Mallon hit his. Both golfers watched the trajectory of the ball as it sailed over the crest and then straight down, followed by a water splash.

"Kerplunk," said Mallon.

"Maybe. Maybe not," said Freddy. "Hold on a minute."

Freddy reached into the side pocket of his golf bag and pulled out a pack of cigarettes.

"Here? Now? You can't wait until we get to the tee?" said Mallon.

Freddy blew out the smoke from the first drag of the cigarette.

"Hey, a man's gotta do what a man's gotta do. Hold on a minute."

Freddy kneeled to tie his already tied shoes.

"Your shoes are tied," said Mallon. "What are you doing?"

"They felt loose on that last shot. Need a tight planting foot," said Freddy kneeling on the ground with his cigarette dangling from his lips while retying his second shoe.

Mallon waited for Freddy when he saw a foursome approaching the tee behind them.

"C'mon, they're going to tee off."

Freddy rose and grabbed his bag.

"Okay, feel much better.  Let's go."

Together they pulled their carts and walked up the rise in the fairway.  Mallon saw his ball where he thought it would be and nodded in approval.  A par was possible.

He saw another ball, about ten yards from the edge of the water which was closer to the green than his ball.  He turned to Freddy.

"That can't be your ball.  I saw a splash."

"I dunno.  I'll have to go check," said Freddy.

"What type of ball are you using?  I'm going with you to check on the ball."

"My, my, Padre.  It's a Titleist 2 for the record.  Your lack of trust borders on appalling."

"Jesus always said, 'Trust but verify,'" said Father Mallon.

"He did not."

"Well, that's what he meant.  It's in the Bible, somewhere."

They walked to the ball where Freddy picked it up, looked at it, and tossed it to Mallon.

"Titleist 2.  Jagoff."

Mallon caught the ball, glanced at it. and flipped it back to Freddy.

"That's Father Jagoff to you."

The front nine ended with Mallon still trailing Freddy but the gap that separated them after the first hole remained steady.

"Let's have a beer," said Freddy as they walked by the clubhouse to start the back nine.

They placed their golf bags on a rack just outside the door and entered.  It took a second for both to adjust to the dark air-conditioned environment as they sat at the bar.

Freddy ordered two Old Styles.  The bartender quickly returned with two sweaty brown longneck bottles.  Freddy took a ten-dollar bill from his pocket and placed it on the bar.  Both took a long drink from their bottles and placed them back on the bar.

"Boy, that hit the spot," said Mallon.

"I heard that," said Freddy.

Freddy took another sip from the bottle and turned to Mallon.

"Remember those nights laying on Mrs. Murray's garage roof during the summer? We'd just lie there, smoking cigarettes and staring up at the stars. You could see a lot more of the sky back then."

"Yeah, I do. Like the time you got sick on those Mulberries and puked your guts out. I remember the purple puke as it rolled down the roof to the alley. Man, that was gross."

"No," Freddy protested. "I think it was those cigarettes more than the Mulberries. We were smoking Lucky Strikes back then, with no filters. Man, that was rough. Juvenile delinquents today are such pussies, their cigarettes have filters on them."

"Nope. It was the berries. That puke river was purple as hell. So, what about it anyway?"

"Well, I remember the night we were up there, and you told me that you were planning on becoming a priest."

Mallon replied, "Yeah, yeah. I think you're right. I remember that."

"Well, that night I also made a career decision."

"Oh yeah?"

"Yeah. It was then that I decided that I would stay with Wally and learn the racket."

"So, you decided on a life of crime that night?"

"Aw, come on Tommy. I didn't look at it as crime. Neither did you."

Mallon nodded his head. Freddy continued. "It was hustling, making a buck. Wally never held up anyone with a gun. He took their money with a smile. I liked that, his style. He was your friend, but he still took your money."

"You mean like you're trying to do to me today?"

A broad grin came over Freddy's face. "Well, yeah. Sorta."

Freddy continued. "But that's what I mean about Wally. He never twisted anyone's arm. No one was ever forced to do anything that they did not want to do. He just gave the people what they wanted." Freddy took another sip of beer and continued. "Let me ask you. Did I twist your arm to bet with me today?"

"No. No, you didn't. It was my choice."

"Exactly."

"So, tell me," said Mallon. "What was the deal with you and Wally? There seemed to be some sort of estrangement between you two."

"Nah, Wally and I got along just fine. For the most part."

"For the most part?"

"Yeah, for the most part," said Freddy. "Do you remember the knife I gave you for your birthday?"

"Yeah, the one with the reindeer carved in the handle? I still have it. It's beautiful."

"Well, he gave me that knife, but for some reason he wanted it back and I said no. He might have gotten a little pissed about that."

"Why would he be pissed about that?"

"I have no idea," said Freddy, "But other than that, we got along fine. I learned a lot from him. Believe me."

Freddy finished his beer and rose from the bar stool.

"C'mon, let's finish this."

Mallon finished his beer and followed Freddy through the door and back outside where they gathered their bags and pull carts and walked to the 10th tee.

"Is it possible for you to enjoy the day and just golf ?" asked Mallon.

"No," said Freddy. "No one golfs for social enjoyment. I heard you swear like a sailor earlier today. That's not social enjoyment. I don't know what you would call it, but it isn't social enjoyment."

"Well, what if I said no to your betting proposition?  Would you still golf with me?"

"Sure.  I guess.  No one has ever said no to me so I can only assume that I would.  But you said yes.  So, it's a moot point.  You tee off first."

Mallon teed his ball up at the par 5 and drove a shot about two hundred yards.  It faded left, just at the edge of the fairway.

Freddy next drove the ball a little past Father Mallon's shot but sliced right.  Together they pulled their carts down the center of the fairway.

"You know, Wally was like a father to me.  Or a big brother.  Whichever is better." Freddy said to Mallon.

The declaration startled him.   "I didn't know that," he said.

"Yeah," said Freddy.  "I looked up to him in a weird way.  The way he did business was something to marvel at."

Mallon laughed as he replied, "You're full of shit, something to marvel at. You don't talk that way.  What are you getting at?"

"Look Tommy, I'm not getting at anything.  I'm telling you something.  Aren't you a priest?  Isn't this what you do?  Listen to people?"

Mallon sensed an opening.  "Sorry.  Go ahead.  I'm listening."

"After you went to the seminary, it was just the two of us and our relationship became a totally different thing."

"Yeah?  How so?"

"Well, I think he trusted me more.  He had to, but he grew more comfortable with me too.  I was making the drops at Sloan's by my-self.  Wally was getting older and anything I could do to get him off his feet, he appreciated," Freddy said.

"So, you got pretty tight with him, didn't you?"

"Well, maybe a little bit after you left for the seminary.  He could give two shits about me before you left."

"Really?  I never noticed that."

Freddy stopped and turned to Mallon. He bowed his head slightly, furrowed his brow and lifted his eyes upward, as a mother would to her son after he said something stupid. "Really?" he said.

"Yeah, really," said Mallon.

"Okay, I'll give you the benefit of the doubt. I get that, but I'm just telling you things from my end, from my point of view. That's all. I already told you that he was like a father to me. He told me he would hold a spot on his crew when I was doing time in the joint. He was taking an interest in me. I appreciated that."

"Let's pick this up on the next tee. I've got to go find my ball," said Mallon. He walked to the edge of the fairway looking for his ball, while Freddy walked ahead to his ball.

Mallon saw his ball laying just off the fairway, about a yard into the rough. He pulled his cart behind where the ball lay and pulled his three-iron from his bag. He turned to address the ball and noticed that Freddy was walking towards the green as if he already took his shot.

That was strange, thought Mallon. Golf courtesy allows the farthest from the green to shoot first. Then it dawned on him that Freddy was up to his shenanigans again. He had let his guard down with the sweet talk about Uncle Wally. Two can play at that game he thought.

Mallon picked up his ball and tossed it on the fairway. He had no intention of taking any penalty this time. He set his feet and aligned his shot, swaying back and forth just like he saw Lee Trevino do in the Masters.

Suddenly thoughts appeared in his head. He was cheating, violating not only the ethics of sportsmanship on the golf course, but defying the ethics of mankind, the social contract with society.

He walked away from the ball and shook his head to shake away any lingering conscience that remained there and took a practice swing. He looked for Freddy, but he was already passed the tree line and out of sight. He addressed the ball again.

And he started to think again.

Was what he was doing just as bad as Freddy? Do two wrongs really make a right? The Big Man is probably looking down at him at this very moment, shaking His holy head in disgust at what His spiritual agent was about to do.

He walked away from the ball again. This time, he picked up his ball and tossed it back into the rough.

He again addressed the ball, but the thoughts returned. He tried to ignore them, and kept his eyes focused on the white orb that lay before him.

Freddy was doing it to him again. But this time he wasn't only taking his money, he was trying to pierce his soul with a lance of memory and sympathy. He was trying to...

He swung his club and watched as the ball traveled all of three feet and bounced into a deeper part of the rough.

...get into his head.

Mallon carded seven shots on the hole.

"You better pick it up on the next eight holes, Padre."

Mallon chuckled and said, "Yeah, you're hustling. Wally would be proud of you."

Freddy smiled and said, "Yeah, I guess he would."

They arrived just as the foursome ahead of them was teeing off, so they sat on a bench to wait their turn.

"You know when I heard what Smitty did to Wally, I cried. I wept like a little fucking baby. I was still in the joint. I should have been there."

Mallon sensed genuine remorse. "I heard that about Smitty just recently. Now that I think about it, I haven't seen him in church in a long while."

Freddy took a cigarette out, lit it and exhaled.

"There's a reason for that," Freddy said as he took another drag.

Mallon turned and looked at Freddy, who was watching the foursome ahead of them on the fairway while working on his cigarette.

"Come on, they're far enough away," said Freddy as he rose and flicked his cigarette away. He grabbed his driver from his bag.

The next four holes were played in silence. Father Mallon found himself less concerned with Freddy's score and more concerned with how he could reach out to him. This wasn't about getting into the good graces of Father Cummins or a Lost Boys Club anymore, he felt a genuine interest in assisting Freddy, someway, somehow.

Of course, Freddy won the hole and the next three. Mallon did not feel the desperation that he thought he would. His concerns were now for Freddy, as he had gone beyond mere hustling. He was on a plateau that was hard to climb down from and easy to fall off. A logarithmically accelerating drop off the sheer cliff of evil with a landing that would not be easy to withstand. Nor to look at.

They teed off on the 17th hole, a par three with a slight dogleg and a green surrounded by sand traps and a grove of trees. It was about 175 yards. A nice poke, but very possible to make a blind landing on the green if you cut over the dogleg, which most people attempted to do.

Freddy was no exception. He hit his ball over the small cluster of trees, right where he wanted and started chirping again.

"Ooh baby. I feel good about that one. Can't wait to see it."

Mallon approached the tee and attempted the same strategy, but he did not clear the trees and a par three was about to turn into a six or seven, but he felt ambivalent about the whole matter. The distraction from Freddy's admission was now complete. Mallon's mind was focusing on other things.

Freddy walked on ahead, eager to see where his ball landed, as Mallon entered the wooded area that abutted every other hole on the course, in what he anticipated would be a futile search for his ball.  But he found it immediately and realized he had a straight shot to the green if he could chip it over the sand trap.  This may not be as bad as he thought.  He took a couple of practice swings with his 9 iron.  He stepped up to the ball then began his backswing.

"HOLY FUCKING SHIT," yelled Freddy from the green.

Mallon chipped the ball directly into the trap.

"What was that?  In the middle of my swing?" yelled Mallon from thirty yards away.

"Sorry.  Sorry, Tommy, but look!" Freddy pointed to the cup on the green.  "I got a fucking hole-in-one!  A hole-in-fucking-one!"

Freddy reached into the cup and pulled out his Titlist Two and held it up.

"See!  See!  No bullshit.  It's my ball!"

"Congratulations.  I'll buy you a beer.  Now let me shoot," said an unimpressed Mallon.

As he entered the sand trap, he noticed a set of footprints where someone had walked through the trap.

"You think those guys would rake the trap," he said.  "Common golf courtesy.  Maybe I'll say something if I see them."

"I wouldn't worry about it," said Freddy.  "Just let it be at that."

Mallon landed a good shot onto the green, about ten feet from the hole.  He two-putted for a five.  It could have been a lot worse, he thought.

As they approached the 18th hole, Freddy had his score card out and was totaling the damage that he was inflicting on Mallon.

"Not as bad as last time.  Only about two hundred bucks."

Mallon shook his head.  He had no words.

"Look, Tommy.  I'm gonna be a nice guy.  I'm feeling good about that ace and everything so, I'll make you an offer."

"I'm listening," said Mallon.

"Double or nothing, winner-take-all on the 18th hole.  I'll even finance it, for a small profit, of course."

They continued to walk, shoulder to shoulder, on the asphalt cart path to the tee box as Mallon mulled Freddy's offer. As they arrived at the tee box, he turned to Freddy.

"Okay, Freddy. I'll accept your offer, but with one additional term."

"Oh yeah? What would that be?"

"If I win this hole, you will also come to Confession this Saturday."

Freddy started to laugh.

"Playing priest with me Tommy? Think you can save my soul? Okay. I'm doing this for you. If you win, I'll go to your ritual this Saturday, but don't expect me to say anything about Smitty. I had nothing to do with it. Really. I don't know if he's dead or just moved to another parish." Freddy's laughter grew. "But I do know I got into your head a little bit, Padre." Freddy's laughter turned into ugly cackle as he reached into his pocket and pulled out a large lug-nut and offered it to Mallon.

"Courtesy of Milly's Apron."

Mallon accepted it and held it in his open palm, bewildered.

"You remember Milly's Apron, don't you Tommy?"

By now Freddy's tone grew more serious. "You remember the wheel rolling off Milly's Apron's sulky as Apple of Mama's Eye roared past to win that last race at Sportsman's? I brought it with me for good luck. It obviously worked. It blew its load for me so maybe there's still something in it for you. Take it Tommy. Every little bit helps."

Mallon looked down at his open hand. He shook his head and thought to himself, "And, I'm trying to save this mother fucker."

A train passed on the tracks parallel to the hole giving him time to formulate a response. He looked back at Freddy, who grinned like an evil cat that ate the canary, so he ran through a speedy Hail Mary and composed himself.

"Let's do this," said Mallon.  He put the lug nut in his pocket. "You're up Freddy boy."

Freddy stepped to the tee, turned to Mallon and smiled.  "You sure about this?"

"Hit the ball," Mallon replied.

Freddy drove his tee shot down the middle of the fairway, over two hundred yards.

"Your turn, Padre."

Mallon walked to the tee, set his feet and adjusted his hips.  He was now technically involved in his swing as he slowly brought his driver back, then rapidly began his downswing, squarely hitting the ball with the sweet spot, driving the ball straighter and farther than Freddy.

The hole was a par four with a slight dogleg right to a huge green between two small sand traps.  Not a difficult hole, Mallon thought. With his long drive, he believed that he could make the green in two and make par with two putts.  With a little luck, he could maybe even birdie the hole.  Freddy would be hard-pressed to beat that.

Freddy shot first from about twenty-five yards behind Mallon and lofted a high shot that bounced in front of the sloping green and rolled on to the lip, about forty feet from the hole.

Mallon let out a small sigh of relief.  In the back of his mind, he imagined Freddy making one of his incredible shots, one that he could actually see.  He grabbed his seven iron.  After two practice swings, he took his shot.  The ball arced perfectly, landing on the green sticking it eight feet from the hole.

He wanted to jump and yell, but instead he glanced at Freddy as he reached into his pocket and wrapped his hand tightly around the lug nut.

Freddy called out.  "Hey, wait up."

Mallon turned and watched as Freddy took out another cigarette and lit it.

"Can't you wait till after we're done?" asked Mallon.

"It calms me down. Big putts coming up," said Freddy as he started making his way to the green.

At the green, they pulled their putters from their bag and walked up the small slope to the green towards the ball that was closest to the hole.

Mallon said, "You know, that's my ball."

"Sorry Padre. That's me. Yours rolled down the slope. It's over there." Freddy pointed to the ball that was just off the green, forty feet away.

"No, no. Check the ball," said Mallon. "That's my ball."

Freddy reached down and grabbed the ball and said, "Titlist Two. That's me Padre."

Mallon wondered how this could be. He had watched as Freddy hit his shot. He watched his own shot. Something was up. He walked down the slope of the green to where the other ball sat. He picked it up and it was indeed his ball, a Top-Flite 4.

The cold slap of reality smacked him in the back of the head. He had been taken to the cleaners. The entire effort to give Freddy spiritual help was a lark.

"Yeah, this is my ball I guess."

"I told you," said Freddy. "You turned around so fast after the shot that you didn't see it roll. And roll. And roll." He started to laugh. "Sorry about that Padre. I can't help it. Some days you got it and some days you got it even more!"

A beaten and emotionally drained Mallon did not respond. He lined up his putt and got it to within fifteen feet of the hole. Three putts later, he found himself three shots behind and looking at the worst financial situation he could have imagined. He was facing some serious discipline, if not total banishment, from the Archdiocese. He would have to resort to again "borrowing" from the parish to pay Freddy. He walked off the green as Freddy lined up his last putt.

He didn't watch Freddy make the putt, but he heard the distinct 'plunk' sound when the ball dropped into the hole.

Next, he heard Freddy yell in triumph, "It's God's Will, Padre!"

He walked towards his cart. Then he heard a dull thud of a hard and heavy object bouncing on the cart path. The next sound Mallon heard was like the sound he heard when he broke Chet Quinlan's baby finger, but this sound was deeper and more resonant.

He turned back towards the green and saw Freddy laying prone, his body twitching and flopping like a goldfish on the floor of a kindergarten class, his face smashed like a collapsed pumpkin three weeks after Halloween.

Then he stopped the flopping and just lay on the green. Dead and bloody.

And without the 400 dollars Mallon owed him.

* * * * * * *

Father Mallon poured himself a glass of scotch and leaned back into his chair. He looked at the heavy object on his bed as a grim smile slowly appeared on his face.

The ambulance had arrived, and they put Freddy and what was left of his face in a large bag, zipped it up and hauled it away. Father Mallon hung around to answer any questions that the police officer on the scene had for him. The officer was interviewing a teen-age boy who had apparently witnessed the incident. Father Mallon did not mind. He had nowhere to go.

Finally, the officer got around to taking Father Mallon's statement. He could only tell the officer what he had heard, as his back was turned when the incident occurred. After he gave his statement, he asked the officer about the boy.

"Oh, him?  He said he was Mr. Gallagher's caddy.  He pretty much confirmed what you said.  He saw a black round object come over the line of trees, bounce on the cart path and hit Mr. Gallagher.  Sounds like a part or something came off the train as it passed by.

"Mr. Gallagher's caddy huh?" said Father Mallon.

"Yeah.  That's what he said.  He said he followed Mr. Gallagher around for the entire round.  Say, didn't you know that?  You were golfing with him, weren't you Father?"

"Yeah, yeah.  I let my caddy go early.  He had to be somewhere."

"Okay, Father.  That'll be it.  Thanks for your help.  This thing looks like a horrible accident."

As he walked to his car from the green, it dawned on Father Mallon that Freddy's "caddy" was the reason Freddy had made his great shots.  The hole in one.  The switching of the balls.  It was a rather elaborate set-up which led Father Mallon to think that he was not the first to get trapped in Freddy's golf web.  He realized that he never had a chance against Freddy, but he did have to admit that Freddy sure smiled a lot during the round.

Father Mallon recalled that he had the best intentions when he teed off on the 1st hole and yet, when he walked off from the 18th hole, he was a defeated and demoralized human.  He wanted to do the right thing, but he had failed, miserably.

Or had he?

He recalled that as he approached his car, he saw a round black object wedged between the front bumper of the car and the curb.

He had bent over to get a better look and he recognized that it was a blood-streaked bowling ball.  He wiped the blood off the insignia of the ball, an AMF Three Dot, and saw the engraved name.

He looked about.  No one looking.  He took the ball and put it the trunk of the car and drove out of the parking lot.

Father Mallon put his glass of scotch on the desk and rose again from his chair.  He walked over to his bed and lifted the towel that covered the blood-stained bowling ball. He stared at the engraved name in the ball. It read: G.O.'D.

# CHAPTER 9

# WEEZER'S SUMMER
# August 1970

The soft morning sounds became harder and more industrial as the sun rose higher. The late summer humidity hung over everything like wet towels draped over a fence to dry. Birds began to chirp in the trees, the sporadic traffic was becoming less so and Mike yelled, softly, at Weezer as they walked along the long line of box cars parked on the tracks that ran north-south over the $67^{th}$ Street viaduct at Bell Avenue.

"Hey, over here. This is the one. I know it."

Weezer caught up to Mike and peered at the box car. He looked at the other box cars and then turned to Mike.

"How is this the one? It looks exactly like all the others."

"I just feel it. I've got some great vibes."

"Vibes? What are you, a fuckin' hippie?"

"Maybe," said Mike as he ran his hand through his shoulder-length dirty dishwater blonde hair that would have to be cut before the school year started the following Monday.

Weezer held up two fingers in a peace sign and replied, "Peace. Now let's find a spike and open this thing."

The two walked about the rocky and weedy ground trying to find a steel railroad spike among the cinders and trash along the tracks. The spike would be used to break the metal seal, which was just a flimsy thin metal band, on the box car. Once the seal was broken, it was just a matter of unlatching the door and sliding it open which would reveal whatever cartage would be there for the taking. Earlier in the week, Weezer had learned that Murph and Rizzo had come across some brand spanking new power tools that would fetch a couple of bucks from Borkie, the neighborhood fence.

Mike found a spike. "Got one," he said as he walked toward the sealed box car door. He inserted the spike into the seal and rotated the spike until it broke. Weezer grabbed the latch handle and after a glance at Mike, flipped it over and slid open the door.

Inside the fully loaded box car were stacks of large cardboard boxes, bigger than each of the boys, all sealed with a GE logo on the side. They were brand-new refrigerators.

"What the hell?" said Weezer. "There's no way we can get these out." He turned to Mike. "You and your vibes. Come on, let's check the next one."

Weezer shut the door and replaced the latch. They walked to the next box car and used the same routine to open it. This time the boxes inside had the Ideal toy logo and were much smaller, maybe three feet by three feet.

And they were also lighter. Weezer grabbed a box and plopped it on the ground where he ripped open the top and found six smaller boxes, each with a transparent piece of plastic on the front which disclosed its content. A Crissy Doll. With the Hair That Grows.

"What the hell is this?" asked Weezer.

"It's a doll. A fucking doll," said Mike.

They stared at their bounty when they heard a distant voice being directed towards them.

"Hey! You kids! Stop!"

They turned and saw a large man, about a half a block away, running towards them and he did not look friendly.

"Shit! Train dicks," said Weezer. "Let's get outta here."

They bolted from the scene but not before Mike grabbed the box of dolls. They beat a path down the sloped embankment to the alley where their bikes were parked. Mike put the box of dolls into the canvas newspaper bag that hung on his bike's handlebars. They pedaled furiously away down the alley, turned onto 67$^{th}$ street and zig-zagged down the side-streets and alleys until they gathered in Weezers back yard.

Stopping in the yard to catch their breath, Weezer turned to Mike.

"What the hell are we going to do with these dolls?"

"What do you mean? I'm going to take them to Borkie," replied Mike. "They gotta be worth something."

"What are you crazy? You want to bring Crissy Dolls to the neighborhood fence? Why don't you just sit on your roof and scream and tell the neighborhood that you're a pussy."

Confusion registered on Mike's face. "What do you mean?"

Weezer shook his head in amazement as to why he had to explain the situation to Mike.

"Look. What did Murph and Rizzo bring to Borkie?"

"Some power tools. I think some socket wrench sets too."

"And what did they get for them?"

"Murph told me five bucks each for the power tools and two bucks for the sockets."

"Okay. That shit sells for over fifty bucks in the stores. At least the power tools do. How much do you think we're going to get for a doll that goes for five bucks in the store? Come on genius, do the math."

Mike's mouth closed as he comprehended what Weezer was trying to tell him.

Weezer continued. "And on top of that, do you really want to peddle hot Crissy Dolls? With the fucking hair that grows?"

Mike got the message. "So, what do we do with them? They're brand new. We can't just throw them out."

Weezer grabbed the box of dolls from Mike's newspaper bag and opened it. He took the six smaller boxes containing the dolls and put three back into Mike's bag.

"Here. Fifty-fifty. Do what you want with them."

* * * * * * * *

The randy mating call of the cicadas grew to a buzzing crescendo as the dusk enveloped the trees. Soon it would be dark, and the cicadas will turn silent until the next day. The darkness also gave Weezer and Mike cover to climb old lady Murray's garage and lay between the roof and the darkness. A Mulberry tree extended its berry laden branches over the garage roof, allowing both Weezer and Mike to lay beneath them and pick berries off the branches while still gazing up into the dark void of space. The fat purple berries were the best. They were lush and plump and juicy. Some even burst as they were picked, gushing the sweet purple juice that would stain their fingers until the next morning. But neither Weezer nor Mike cared. They each lay fully sated from the berries on the slanted garage roof with their now purple fingers interlocked behind their heads as pillows, enjoying the view into infinity and the periodic evening breeze.

Weezer turned to Mike. "Got any smokes?"

Mike reached into his front pants pockets. "I think so." He pulled out a mangled pack of Kents and investigated the pack. "Yeah, there's a couple in here."

Mike pulled out the first cigarette and it immediately broke in half. Cigarettes in soft packs do not survive well in the front pocket of adolescent blue jeans. He pulled a second and third one out, the last of the pack, both were a bit crooked but smokable. He crumbled the empty pack and tossed it over the edge of the roof.

Then he reached back into his pocket, pulled his empty hand out and tried his other pocket. Still nothing. "Shit," he said. "You got any matches?"

Weezer reached into his front pocket and pulled out a contorted book of matches. He flipped open the cover and glanced at the supply.

"Only two matches left. Better make it count."

Weezer handed the matchbook to Mike, who took the book and pulled off the first match. He struck it on the back-side scratch strip of the matchbook and ignited the head only to have it go out immediately from a wisp of the evening breeze.

"Dumbass. You know you're supposed to cup it," said an exasperated Weezer.

Mike grabbed the last match from the book.

"Don't fuck it up," ordered Weezer.

Feeling the pressure, Mike put his cigarette in his mouth, struck the match and immediately stuck the end of the cigarette into the still flaring match head, breathing in the sulfur from the match along with the tobacco. The cigarette ignited as he took in far more smoke than he had intended and started to hack and cough.

"Shhh," said Weezer as he laughed at Mike. "Old lady Murray will be out here if you don't shut it."

Mike tried to silence his reaction, which made the matter worse and brought up a large wad of phlegm that he spit off the side of the roof. He collected himself and handed Weezer his smoke. Weezer took it and used the lit end to light his own. Weezer took a light drag from his cigarette.

"See, the trick is Mike, to just drag on it until the tip lights up. Watch."

Weezer took a hit of his smoke while watching the tip light up. He immediately removed the smoke from his lips, inhaled, and let out a small wisp of smoke.

"See.  No muss no fuss."

Mike put his smoke to his lips and followed Weezer's routine. He let out the smoke and laid back down on the roof. "Yeah.  Yeah, I get it now."

Both boys stared into the night sky.  The evening was cloudless with a bright moon.  The stars were also out, at least as many as you can see from a city-lit garage roof on a moonlit night, some brighter than others, some twinkled and some did not.  The boys laid there, occasionally taking a light hit from their cigarettes.  Finally, Weezer broke the silence.

"Back to school on Monday."

"Shit," said Mike. "I forgot."

"I don't mind," said Weezer. "I'm ready.  I'm bored."

"What is wrong with you man?  You want to have to get up at seven every morning now?  Homework?  Nuns yelling at you all the time?"

"I hate all that.  But we are going to be in the eighth grade this year.  We are going to run things.  Plus, I want to see some people I haven't seen all summer."

"Like who?"

"Cindy Pornetelli."

"Porno?"

"Yeah, I bet her tits are out to here now."  Weezer extended his arms and cupped his palms about two feet from his chest.

"Who else?" continued Mike.

"Hm.  Let me think.  Oh, I know, Susan Callahan got a nice little ass that I want to see."

Mike snickered as he responded. "What? Her ass? That's gross man."

"What's so gross about it?"

"That's where you shit, man. Disgusting."

"Well you piss out of your dick."

"That's different."

"What's so different about it?"

"Well, for one thing, shit is nastier than piss. You get some piss on your hand and it's no big deal, you just wash it off, but if you get shit on your hand, you act crazy to get it off. Like you got a deadly spider on your hand or something."

Mike took another drag from his cigarette and exhaled a small burst of smoke.

"Anyway, I'm a tit man myself," he said as if he knew what he was talking about.

Weezer laughed loudly. "You've never gotten any tit!"

"How do you know if I got any tit or not?"

"When? When have you ever got any fuckin' tit?"

"Social Center at Raster. Slow dancing with Megan Stewart."

"Social Center?"

"Yeah. We were slow dancing, and I kept my elbow on her right tit and she didn't move it away. I had my elbow on her tit for almost the whole song."

"Whoa. I didn't know that. How was it?"

"It was great. She even smiled at me after the dance."

They both took another small drag from their cigarettes. Mike blew his out directly, while Weezer let out a continuous flow of smoke-rings until his supply diminished. Mike was impressed.

"Wow. Nice rings man."

"No big thing. You just snap your jaw. Watch."

Weezer took another drag from his cigarette, this time a little deeper, blew out some smoke and then snapped his jaw five or six times to form and expel the smoke rings from his mouth. The perfectly formed smoke rings burst from his mouth and hung in the air until they slowly dissipated in the light breeze.

Mike took a hit from his cigarette and tried to emulate Weezer's skill in blowing smoke rings but to no avail. Mike didn't snap his jaw properly and the smoke came out of his mouth like burps from a '63 Biscayne that needed a carburetor adjustment.

"Hey, man, you've been smoking at least a month before I was. I'll catch up."

The two boys continued gazing into the night sky and enjoyed the last drags from their cigarettes. After which they flicked them off the side of the roof and into the alley.

Weezer broke the silence.

"So, what are you going to do with your Chrissy Dolls?"

"Well, I gave one to the dog. He had fun pulling the hair out and tossing it around the yard until its head came off. The other two I think I'll just save for the fourth and blow them up. You?"

"I don't know," said Weezer while still staring upwards. "They're under my porch in a plastic bag. Can't sell them."

"Well save them for the fourth. Bring them over to my house. We'll put an M-80 in her head and watch it blow to smithereens. It will be fun."

"We'll see. You got any more smokes?"

"No. Those were the last ones," answered Mike.

"That's okay. I was thinking of cutting back anyway."

"Cutting back? How many do you smoke a day?"

"Oh, maybe two or three."

"Packs?"

"No, cigarettes."

"Well, maybe that will be good for you."

Mike reached up to the tree branch that dangled above both their heads and pulled off a clump of mulberries. He offered some to Weezer.

"Want one?"

"No. I'm done. I can't eat too many of those things."

"Well, I can," said Mike as he picked some choice berries from the group and popped them into his mouth. "Juicy fuckers," he said as the purple mulberry nectar bled down his chin. "I can eat these things all night."

"Be careful with that shit. If you eat too many, you'll get a stomachache."

"Don't worry, my stomach can handle it," said Mike as he ate more of the berries.

"Did I tell you that my old man caught me smoking the other night?"

"No." replied Mike.

"Yeah, I was in the alley, behind the garage when he came out with the garbage. He saw me right away. Couldn't ditch the thing."

"Was he pissed?"

"Hell yeah. He grabbed the smoke out of my hands and smacked me across the back of my head. Hurt like hell."

"Wow."

"Man, you're lucky that you don't have an old man."

"What?"

Weezer tried to clarify his statement. "You know what I mean," he paused. "What's it like anyway? Is it weird?"

After a pause and a deep sigh, Mike responded. "It's normal. I don't know any other way. My Dad split when I was two years old. It's not weird. It's normal. Which is kinda weird in itself."

Weezer now regretted his earlier comment, but he felt that he could not just bail on Mike. "So, weird is normal. I get it."

Mike appreciated Weezer's grasp of the issue as they both continued their gaze into the dark heavens for a silent minute.  He sensed Weezer's awkwardness with the conversation and changed the subject and tone.

"So, what are you going to be when you grow up?"

"I dunno.  Maybe I'll follow my old man to Continental Can, like my brother Tim, but he tells me he hates it.  So maybe not.  You?"

"My mother thinks I should work for the city."

"Doing what?"

"I don't know.  She keeps talking about the security of a city job and the retirement benefits.  I just can't think of that shit, not now anyway.  Anyway, I still want to play first base for the White Sox."

"Well, hey.  You never know.  Now don't get a big head or anything, but you're a pretty good first baseman in Little League."

The unexpected compliment raised Mike's spirits a notch.

"Thanks," said Mike as he sat up and exposed the true extent of juice stains around his lips, much to Weezer's amusement who started to laugh.

"Look at you!  You looked like you sucked off a Martian!"

Realizing without seeing what he must look like, Mike tried to wipe the purple residue with the arm of his shirt, but only smeared it, which prompted more comments from Weezer.

"That didn't help.  You still look like you sucked off a Martian, but in a windstorm!"

"Ah, who gives a shit," responded Mike.  "Nobody's going to see it anyway."

"I wish I had a camera.  Your mug is classic."

Mike laid back down, not particularly amused.

"Hey man, lighten up.  Think about it, you'll be playing first base for the Sox, and I'll be at Continental Can."

"Ha, yeah," said Mike. "You'll have to come to me for free tickets." He smiled at the thought. "But you don't have to work at the Can, do you?"

"I guess not. But what else am I going to do? I really think that the old man wants me to work at the Can. I really do."

"Did he tell you that?"

"No. I just sense it from him. I don't think he cares, to tell you the truth. The Can thing is just a fall back, I think. It's been a couple of years now, and I still don't think he's over Greg getting killed in Viet Nam. He just hasn't been the same."

"How so?"

"Well, I've never seen a man cry so much in my life. We'll be talking or something and I'll say Greg's name or something that reminds him of Greg, and he just turns it on like a water faucet."

"I feel sorry for the guy. I really do," said Mike.

"I do too. I know he is hurting, it's obvious. His whole personality is different from what it was. What I remember it to be. Yeah, he's hurting, but so am I. He's like a ghost. He's there, but he isn't. You know that your father is gone. I don't know if mine is. He's around but he's not. Weird is becoming normal."

Mike sat up and looked at Weezer, as if he had a deep profound retort. He opened his mouth to speak his wisdom when a thick stream of purple projectile vomit blasted simultaneously from his nose and mouth.

Fortunately for him, Weezer saw the oncoming barrage a split second before he would have been the subject of a direct hit and leaned back as the torrent of purple vomit shot over his chest and onto the roof beside him where it flowed down the roof's shingles and onto the alley below.

The color seemed to return to Mike's face as he spit out the last bits of puke and started to slide down the roof. Weezer laughed.

"I'm going home," said Mike. "I'll see you tomorrow."

"Are you alright?" Weezer asked.

Mike threw a wave toward Weezer and repeated "I'll see you tomorrow."

Weezer waved back and laid back down on the roof looking into the night sky.  His mind was a blank page, which he found relaxing.  Suddenly the faint image of a shooting star raced through the night sky.  Weezer had never seen a shooting star before.

"Wow!" said Weezer.  "Did you see that?"

He turned to where Mike had been sitting and looked about for anyone.  Anyone he could tell what he had just seen.  But nobody was there.

# CHAPTER 10

# BACK TO SCHOOL
## September 1970

The array of blue congregated in the schoolyard. All the students at St. Justin were required to wear the school uniform, which for the boys consisted of a light blue shirt with a navy-blue tie and pants. The girls wore a navy-blue jumper over a white blouse. The uniforms were fresh and crisp. The shoes and belts were new and would be broken in over the course of a week or two. The local uniform store, Gately's, had made their annual haul and not until the first day of school next year would the schoolyard occupants look so new and shiny.

The first through fourth grade lined up in front, while the older students, fifth through eighth grades amassed in the rear schoolyard. The parents of the first graders, mostly mothers, stood next to their apprehensive children while they awaited instructions from the nuns and teachers as to what the procedure was for the children to line up and enter the school.

There were not any parents present of the older students who milled about in familiar groups and swapped summer stories of baseball, vacations, and far-fetched youthful romances.

Weezer and Mike were gathered with Bullethead, Billy Duffy and Pat Gibbons in a small circle near the first mobile unit.

"We spent a week at the Dells. Rode the Ducks and saw the Tommy Bartlet Water Circus. There were some hot babes, man. These chicks in their bathing suits. Whew!" said Billy Duffy.

"Did you fuck any of them?" asked Pat Gibbons.

"No," admitted Billy. "But I swear one of them was checking me out while she was skiing by me."

"Oh yeah, right," said Pat.

Just then Mickey Doty approached the group and slotted himself between Weezer and Mike.

"Hey guys. Here we go again, huh?" said Doty.

Weezer looked down at the pants that Doty had on. They were the proper shade of navy-blue but there was something different about them. The pant legs flowed down and widened at the bottom, which covered half the shoe Doty had on each foot.

"Are those bell bottoms?" asked Weezer in an accusatory tone.

"No," said Doty defensively.

"Bell bottoms? You pussy!" exclaimed Pat Gibbons.

Duffy reached over with his foot and touched the bottom of each leg. "Ding. Dong," he said.

"They're not bell bottoms!" said Doty. "They're flairs. There's a difference."

"Oh, yeah?" said Weezer. "What's the difference?"

"Bell bottoms are bigger. Flairs are smaller."

"That just makes you a small pussy," said Gibbons.

"Yeah," chimed in Mike. "You're a small little pussy!" The entire group broke out in spontaneous laughter at Mike's clever line. Mike, who was not familiar with having his attempts at humor succeed, looked about to verify that he was not the subject of the laughter, and laughed louder and longer than anyone in the group.

"Okay, Mike. That's enough," said Bullethead.

Mike quickly ceased his over-the-top laughter but not pursuant to Bullethead's order, for he had focused in on a new teacher that was talking with another group of students in the corner of the yard.

"Whoa," said Mike. "She's a babe."

The entire group visually followed Mike's focus and a momentary silence came over them. They were studying the new teacher.

She was a young blonde, who wore a short bob hairdo and had on a summer dress that flowed about her like satin sheets, or so thought Mike.

"Man, I hope I'm in her home room. I could stand looking at that every morning," Mike said as he stared at his own perfect vision of loveliness.

Weezer wasn't having any of it. "You wouldn't know where to start."

The group chuckled and Mike turned defensive, again.

"What do you know?" Mike grabbed his crotch. "I'd having her begging for more all night."

The group collectively moaned and laughed at Mike's juvenile braggadocio.

It was then that the ancient Sister Bernadette clad in her starched black and white habit rang the hand bell that signaled that it was time to enter the school. The students lined up according to the grade they were in and then each teacher or nun stood at the head of the class that they oversaw.

As Weezer and Mike approached their line, Mike turned to Weezer, "So what's up after school? We only have a half-day today."

From twenty feet away, Sister Bernadette chastised Mike.

"Mr. Raskin, be quiet. Talking time is over."

"Yes, Sister," said Mike as he got into line.

It was then that the new teacher with the blonde bob came to the eighth-grade line. Mike was elated.

"Hell, yeah," he whispered to Weezer. "I'm gonna have a boner every morning."

"Shut up, would you?" said Weezer.

The lines started to move through the side doors of the building. Each line was directed by the teacher or nun to their classrooms where the students took their seats, unassigned for now, and prepared for the first day of the school year.

Mike and Weezer entered room eight with the rest of their class and took their seats in the rows of immovable desks. Mike sat directly behind Weezer as he settled down to hear the opening remarks from his babe of a teacher. She stood before the class.

"Good morning and welcome," she said in a delightful voice that Mike anticipated. "As some of you know, there have been some changes for this year. For the first time, some of us will not be wearing our habits, so let me write my name on the blackboard."

She started to write her name in cursive with a brand-new piece of chalk. When she was done, she turned around and moved to the side to allow everyone to see her name.

She wrote, "Sister Marie."

Mike saw the name on the blackboard and started to turn white. He leaned forward and whispered to Weezer, "She's a fuckin' nun?"

Weezer turned and glanced at Mike's ashen face. "Yeah, I guess so," he said as he tried to conceal his laughter. But he couldn't.

"Young man, what is so funny? Stand up and tell me your name," said Sister Marie.

Weezer realized that she was talking to him, so he stood up. "My name is Gary O'Donnell, and I was trying to help my sick friend here, Mike Raskin." He pointed to Mike.

"Oh?" said Sister Marie. "Young man, don't you feel well?"

Mike just shook his head.  Sister Marie looked at the paleness of his face and grabbed a garbage can from the corner of the room and approached Mike with it.

"If you're sick, use this.  Don't worry."

Sister Marie put the garbage can in the aisle next to Mike and laid her soft and gentle hand on the back of his head which she started to caress.  Mike immediately threw up his breakfast into the garbage can.  Weezer could not hold in his laughter which earned him a stern condemnation from Sister Marie.

"This is not funny Mr. O'Donnell.  This poor young man may be very sick."  She turned back to Mike and laid her hand back on his head and stroked his hair.  He threw up again.

"Oh, you poor thing," said Sister Marie.

With his face still in the garbage can, Mike replied, "I'll be alright, Sister.  I'm feeling better now."  He spit out the remaining bits of vomit and wiped his mouth with his shirtsleeve.  He sat up and asked for permission to go to the lavatory to clean up.

"Of course," said Sister Marie.  "Mr. O'Donnell, go with him please and make sure he's alright."

"Yes, Sister," said Weezer.  He held out his hand to assist Mike from his desk. They left the classroom.

As they got into the hallway, Weezer turned to Mike, "Are you okay?"

"Yeah, yeah.  I'm fine.  It just threw me when she said she was a nun."

"So that's what it's like to want to do a nun, huh?"

"Shut up," said Mike.

After Mike rinsed out his mouth in the lavatory and Weezer relieved himself, they returned to the class.  Sister Marie noted their return.

"How are you feeling Mr. Raskin?"

"I'm fine Sister. I'm fine," said Mike as he and Weezer sat back down at their desks.

"Very well then," said Sister Marie. "You are back in time for the welcoming from Pastor Cummins."

It was then that the speaker above the blackboard came alive and the voice of Pastor Cummins, came through the speaker.

"Good morning, children. Welcome to the new schoolyear. It's good to see all your faces again for another year of fun and learning."

After a series of boring announcements, Father Cummins led the school in prayer.

A solemn Sister Bernadette was next. She said a prayer for the souls that God had called home.

"Sixth grader Eddie Crane's grandfather passed away in July. Rest in Peace."

"Susan Callaghan's mother lost her fight with breast cancer in early August. Rest in Peace."

Sean O'Brien was hit by a car while coming home from mass in June. Rest in Peace.

Holy shit, thought Weezer. Sean O'Brien is dead? He turned around and looked at Mike, who was busy doodling drawings of what he thought were anatomically correct breasts.

"Did you hear that?" whispered Weezer.

"Hear what?" whispered Mike.

"Sean O'Brien's dead."

Sister Marie was witnessing the conversation.

"Mr. O'Donnell, eyes forward."

Weezer turned around and stared straight ahead. His eyes did not focus on anything. They could not.

The two boys started the two-block walk home from school after a half-day. The mass of students that exited the school doors dispersed in many directions. Eventually, Weezer and Mike were walking by themselves down Honore Street. Mike looked about and enjoyed the trees that were starting to change and the high sun of a beautiful sky.

Weezer was preoccupied mulling over the possibility of eternal damnation from God and the effect it would have on the rest of his life.

Just then, a White on Black 1967 Chevrolet Impala slowly drove by.

"Wow," said Mike. "I could pick up some chicks in that."

He turned to Weezer. "Did you see that?"

"No, what?" said Weezer.

"The car. The Impala. It was a thing of beauty."

"No, must have missed it," muttered Weezer.

"What's up with you? Where's your head?"

"Sean O'Brien's dead."

"Yeah, we know that."

"I didn't know that."

"You didn't? I ran into his brother at the park over the summer. He told me everything. Got hit by a car crossing 71st Street coming home from a mass that he had served."

"Do you know when?"

"Well, it had to be in June sometime. I met his brother at a Fourth of July party at the park."

"Would it have been the mass we served with him? When we took the money?"

"I don't know. Maybe. What's that matter?"

"Nothing. I hope."

They came to their fork in the road where Mike would short-cut to his house on Hermitage and Weezer would continue down Honore.

"Fast-Pitching?" Mike said as he started down the alley.

"Yeah," said Weezer. "See you back in the school yard in about a half hour. Let me go home and change."

Fast-Pitching (or Strikeout, per some heretics), is a game where two people can play baseball, mano-a-mano, and announce their presence with authority.  All that was needed was a bat, a rubber ball and an area large enough where any windows would be out of range, which the schoolyard at St. Justin certainly qualified.  The rubber balls came in two sizes, regular and small.  The balls had fake seams imprinted on them, so one could grip the ball like the pitchers on the baseball cards.  After the first inning, the paint on the ball would start to flake off, and small white particles would blow about and then be gone forever.

A box would be chalked or painted, depending on the level of delinquency of the artist, on the wall of a building.  This was the strike zone.  The object was to attempt to blow your best fastball past the batter standing in front of the box.  If the hitter made contact, there were parameters based on the distance the ball was hit which would determine if it was a single, or extra base hit.

Weezer, Mike and the group had spent many afternoons throwing these rubber balls against the brick walls of the rectory garage.  These practices were encouraged and endorsed by the parish as displayed by the water fountain they had installed on the far wall of the garage.

By the time Weezer and Mike arrived back at the schoolyard, there was a bit of a crowd.  Two Fast-Pitching games were already in progress and a group of younger students were gathered by the mobile units playing hopscotch and jumping rope.

The playground at St. Justin was not a playground.  It was a parking lot that was filled every Sunday morning with the automobiles of worshippers, but during the week it served as a place of congregation for the players of games that required a good amount of space in an urban neighborhood.  In addition, three shiny new mobile units occupied the southern corner of the lot and now served not only as places of parochial instruction but as great make-out sites as the stairs of the units here hidden and comfortable.

"I'll bat first," said Weezer as he grabbed his bat and took his position at the last box available at the left side of the garage wall. Mike took his position at the pitcher's mound, which was universally agreed to be aligned with the telephone pole off to the side of the schoolyard.

Mike fired his first pitch outside of the box, ball one. He wound up and threw his next pitch, a strike that hit the line of the box on the outside edge. Strike one.

"Come on, pussy. Throw me the ball," said Weezer.

Mike's next pitch came directly at Weezer, who managed to get out of the way.

"Okay, okay," said Weezer. "You want to play that game."

Mike wound up and delivered another pitch. Weezer got all of it and sent it out of the schoolyard, over the street where it landed two backyards deep across the street from the schoolyard. A home run.

"Crap!" yelled Mike.

Weezer smugly waived to Mike. "Bye-bye."

Not only had Mike delivered the pitch that was sent rocketing out of the schoolyard, but he also had to go and fetch the ball. Hopefully there was not a dog in the yard.

Weezer took a few practice swings while he waited for Mike to return. Then he sat down in the shade of the garage shadow and noticed a middle-aged man enter the yard. He had on a white shirt that had seen its better days, and a black tie with the knot hanging on the man's chest. He wore wire spectacles and held a Bible in his hand. His combover hairstyle flopped back and forth as he staggered into the yard. It was obvious that the man had been drinking.

"You kids should be in prayer!" the middle-aged man yelled as he held his Bible in the air.

All the games in the schoolyard came to a halt as the players turned their attention to the man.

"You're all a bunch of sinners!" he exclaimed.  Then he stopped in the middle of the schoolyard and looked directly at an open page of the Bible.  The hand he held the Bible with, his left, had a severely bent little finger.

"Godly grief produces a repentance that leads to salvation without regret, whereas worldly grief produces death," he said and then looked up at the scared, curious, and irate students in the schoolyard.

"You must repent," he yelled.  He turned and looked directly at Weezer, or so Weezer thought, and continued, "Or you WILL GO TO HELL!"

Weezer wasn't having it.  "No, you go to Hell, you old drunk!" he screamed back.

The old man turned to Weezer and started to walk towards him in a slow unsteady gait.  Weezer rose with his bat in his hand and the old man stopped and turned to his open Bible.  He clumsily flipped the pages of the book until he found what he was looking for and then turned back to Weezer, while holding his right hand in the air.

"When a man's ways are pleasing to the Lord, he makes even his enemies be at peace with him.  Proverbs chapter 16 verse 7."

After a pause, Weezer said, "When a drunk comes up to you, grab a bat.  Weezer, September 1970."

Even in his inebriated state, the old man realized that he was facing a potentially dangerous scenario.  He stood as best as he could and reached into his pants pocket and pulled out his handkerchief. He wiped his brow.

"Man, it's hot out here," he said.  He closed his Bible and walked over to the shaded area by the mobile units and sat on the metal steps, while continuing to wipe his brow.

Father Mallon opened the door to the rectory. There he found Cindy Rizzo and Mary Bartholomew, both sixth grade students at the school.

"Father, the Finger Man is in the playground bothering us again," said Cindy.

"Yeah, Father. He's saying bad words and things," added Mary.

"Who is this Finger Man?" asked Father Mallon.

"He's a drunk old man who keeps saying that we're all going to burn in the fires of hell," said Cindy. "Sorry Father, but he is really scary."

"C'mon, show me this Finger Man," replied Father Mallon as he followed the two girls to the playground.

Father Mallon walked out from the rectory and into the schoolyard, where he found the Finger Man, sitting on the stairs of the mobile unit in the afternoon shade, holding his wire-frame spectacles with his left hand and wiping his brow with his right hand. The handkerchief hid his face from Father Mallon, but Mallon knew who he was when he saw the crooked pinky on his right hand.

"Chet. Get up."

Chet Quinlan put his spectacles on and after a couple of quick winks, focused on the figure standing before him. It took him a long second, but he recognized the face and immediately rose from the stairs and held his hands up.

"Sorry, Tommy."

"Put your hands down, Chet," said Father Mallon. Some of the children were still gathered around to watch the inevitable clash between good and evil. This limited the conversation he could have with Chet. "C'mon, let me take you home."

Chet obeyed Father Mallon's request and followed him as they walked through the gauntlet of children and out of the playground.

They got into Father Mallon's Torino.

"Chet, what are you doing out there?  You're scaring the kids."

"Well, someone has to save these children.  They're all going to hell in a handbasket.  They're out here playing around when they should be at home praying to Jesus."

Father Mallon felt a familiar old burn rise in his body.  He closed his eyes and silently started to pray the Hail Mary.  He stopped halfway through and turned to Chet and gestured to the collar on his shirt.

"Chet, do you see this collar I have on?" he said in a low, simmering voice.

"Yes.  Yes, I do Father."

"Do you know what that means, Chet?"

"It means you're a man of God."

"Right.  Exactly, Chet," the simmer was rising to a pre-boil.  "And that means ONLY I CAN TELL SOMEONE THEY'RE GOING TO HELL AROUND HERE!"

Chet's eyes widened and he listened intently.

"Now, I do not want to see you in this playground ever again," continued Father Mallon.  "Do you understand that, Chet?"

Chet nodded.  He pulled out his handkerchief and started to wipe his brow again.

"If I see you in this playground again and there are children around, I will give you matching pinkies. You don't want that, do you Chet?"

Chet shook his head.

"No, Chet.  I want you to say it out loud.  That you will never come back to this playground again."

"I will..."

Father Mallon bobbed his head in the rhythm that Chet had started as he helped Chet get the words out.

"C'mon now Chet. Say it.  I will not..."

"I will not," Chet swallowed as if he was eating oysters for the first time and slowly continued "come to the playground anymore."

"Thank you, Chet. Now where do you live?"

"Seventy-First Street, just off Wolcott."

Father Mallon started the car and backed out of the driveway, onto Honore and then hung a right. In two minutes, he pulled in front of Chet's residence, which was a nice frame single family home.

"Are you going to need some assistance, Chet?"

"No, no. I'm good Tommy, er, Father," said Chet as he fell out of the car and onto the curb.

Father Mallon exited the car and walked around to where Chet lay like a drunken turtle on its back, limbs attached to a large mass futilely moving about in desperate animation. Father Mallon let out a small laugh and bent over to help him.

"C'mon Chet, get up. Let's get you inside."

With Father Mallon holding on to his arm, Chet shakily rose and slowly made his way to the sidewalk. Father Mallon attempted to steer him to the front entrance of the house, but Chet led him to the gangway where he would enter the basement through the rear door.

"This is the way I get in and out," said Chet as he led Father Mallon through the gangway. They entered the yard and Chet walked down some steps and inserted a key into the door. Swinging the door open, he beckoned Father Mallon in.

"Welcome to my humble abode, Father."

Father Mallon walked into what was the basement of the home, made comfortable as a living space with a couch, a bed, a television set, and a bathroom with shower.

"Sit down Father. Can I get you a beer or something?"

"No, I'm good. I've got to get back."

Chet went to the bathroom area and started peeing in the toilet. If there was a door, he did not utilize it.

Father Mallon looked about the living quarters. It seemed that Chet was surviving well.

"Who lives upstairs?" Father Mallon said loudly out of curiosity.

"My sister, Claire. She and her husband," Chet said as he reached for a bottle of brown liquor that was on the kitchen table. He grabbed a glass from the sink, rinsed it and brought the glass to the table. He lifted the bottle to pour into the glass when he paused.

"Say, you and Claire had a thing before, didn't you?"

"You can say that," said Father Mallon.

Chet continued his pour. "Boy, I forgot about that. She'll be happy to see you. I'll go get her, she's just upstairs."

"No, no, Chet. That's alright."

Chet took a long sip from the brown liquor. "You sure? It's not a big thing. I'm sure she's upstairs right now."

Father Mallon gave it a quick thought and decided against it.

"No, I'm going to go. But you listen to what I told you about going to the playground anymore. I meant it, Chet."

"Yeah, yeah. I got you Father. I'll just go over to Raster School and preach to the public kids. Those kids are a bunch of heathens. Publics. Who needs 'em."

"Fine. Take that crap to the publics, they need it," said Father Mallon as he turned to walk out.

As he exited the basement door, he walked up the short flight of steps to ground level and found that the entire yard was filled with a colorful array of hung laundry that waived in the slight breeze. There was clothing of various types, towels, and a variety of children's attire, both boys and girls, that ranged in sizes.

And then there was Claire.

Father Mallon stopped in his tracks. He had thought of Claire many times in the past twelve years, and she was exactly how he had envisioned her. The radiant glow that evidenced the rapturous qualities of a younger woman that he had remembered was still there.

The swaying laundry took turns hiding and then exposing her as she hummed a song while she hung the clothes on the line. He did not recognize the song, but he started to hum along anyway.

At first, Claire did not see where the accompanying humming was coming from, but she kept going, probably hoping to be surprised by one of her children or maybe even her husband coming home from work early. She eventually homed in on the source and moved aside a hanging fitted sheet and found herself looking directly at Father Mallon.

There was a moment of silence. Not an awkward silence, but a silence that allowed each of them to look at each other and comprehend a past that they had both figured they would never need to recall.

They both grinned sadly. They were aware that what could have been will never be.

"How are you, Claire?" said Father Mallon.

"I'm fine Tommy." She paused and continued, "I can still call you that, right?"

"Yes. You sure can," said Father Mallon, smiling again while walking towards Claire. He attempted to give her a quick hug, but the fitted sheet drifted between them. Both started to laugh, and the quick hug was completed.

Father Mallon stepped back and displayed his attire. "Well, it's pretty obvious what I did since we last met. How about you? How's things?"

"Well, I met Ed, he's a cop. We've been married for almost ten years now. We have two wonderful sons and knock-on-wood, everything is good."

"Are they students at St. Justin?"

"No, no. They go to Raster. Sorry to say, we haven't been to church in a while."

"That's quite alright. It happens. Well, I just brought Chet home. He was scaring the kids in the school yard."

"Again? I'll have Ed talk with him."

"It may not be necessary. We had a pleasant chat."

Father Mallon glanced at his watch. "Well, I have to get back to the church. It was nice seeing you."

"I'll walk you out to the car," said Claire as she tossed the clothes pins she was holding into the laundry basket.

They turned and walked single file through the gangway, Father Mallon in front.

"So how long has Chet been with you?"

"Oh, probably about four or five years now. He's still the same Chet that you knew, except for this God thing. I don't know where that came from."

"Well, I guess you can say the same thing about me."

Claire smiled. "I didn't mean that."

They got to the front of the house and Father Mallon walked to the driver's side door. Claire stayed on the sidewalk. As Father Mallon was about to enter the car, he asked Claire, "So just for my curiosity's sake, why didn't you show up at the Berghoff?"

Claire looked down and approached the car.

"I tried. I thought long and hard about us. I did go. I went to meet you. I got downtown a little early, so I was doing some window shopping and as I was walking down Randolph, from out of no-where, I was hit in the head with a pie. It knocked me out and I was in the hospital for three days, in and out of consciousness."

Claire interpreted the ashen look on Father Mallon's face as one of disbelief.

"I know it sounds crazy, but it is the truth. I swear it."

Father Mallon looked down at the keys he was holding in his hand. He switched them from hand-to-hand numerous times and then looked up at Claire.

"I believe you," he said. He could not decide what to say after that. "I have to go now," was all he could come up with. He opened the door to the car, got in and drove off.

Claire watched the car until it disappeared.

Father Mallon pulled his car into the driveway and turned the engine off. He sat in the car and tried to recall what Claire had told him, word for word.

Early. Meet You. Randolph. Pie.

"It was Freddy's pie, just let it be at that," he said and exited the car.

He would normally enter directly into the rectory, but today he thought it would be a good idea to peek into the schoolyard to make sure there was not any more excitement for the day. He walked through the narrow way and into the schoolyard, which was empty but for Weezer, sitting alone in the long shadow of the garage with his baseball bat beside him.

Weezer did not see or hear Father Mallon enter the schoolyard. He looked as if he was in some sort of deep thought or trance. Father Mallon got to within ten feet of him before a startled Weezer noticed him.

"Whoa, sorry Father. You scared me there."

"Sorry," said a smiling Father Mallon. "I did not mean to scare you. What are you doing?"

"Oh, just thinking," said Weezer.

"That's cool. Thinking is good."

"Yeah, sometimes you just have to sit to a have a good think," said Weezer. "You know, thinking is like bowling."

"How so?"

"Well, when you're up at the line, ready to bowl, you have to focus. Where you're aiming. How you throw the ball. You need to pay attention. Thinking is like that. Nobody around to distract you. Real quiet. You get some good thinking done that way."

"Well that certainly makes sense," said Father Mallon. "What are you thinking about?"

"Oh, nothing."

"Well, you are thinking of something. Come on, tell me."

Still sitting, Weezer stared at the tips of his tennis shoes. He clicked them together three times and said, "Whether I'm going to Hell or not."

"What makes you feel like you're going to Hell?"

"Oh, I don't know."

"Did that old man scare you out here? Don't worry, he won't be by again."

"No, he didn't scare me.  I had my bat. I wasn't scared."

"What did he say to you?"

"That I'm going to Hell.  I just wonder how he knew."

"Listen, Mr. O'Donnell, or Weezer. That's it, right?  That's what they call you?"

"Yeah."

"Listen, Weezer.  You are not going to Hell. Trust me on this one."

"Then why did he say it?"

"He's an old man who drinks too much.  He needs help."  Father Mallon knelt beside Weezer and looked him in the eyes.

"Are you going to believe him or me?"

"You."

"That's what I thought you'd say.  It's getting late, Weezer. Shouldn't you be making your way home for supper?"

"Yeah, you're right Father," said Weezer as he rose from his sitting position.

"Okay, Weezer, see you tomorrow," said Father Mallon as he walked away to the rectory.

Weezer took his bat and carried it over his shoulder as he made the walk home. Despite Father Mallon's assurances, he was still concerned about his possible track to Hell.

He could not get Sean O'Brien out of his mind.  He felt somehow responsible for Sean's death.  He tricked Sean into taking the money from the sacristy.  He took the money from Sean after telling him a whopper. Sean probably got all out of whack once he realized what he did, wasn't paying attention, got whacked by a car. Yeah, he was going to Hell.

He wondered what his mother would make for supper. He was hungry.

# CHAPTER 11

# HALLOWEEN
## October 1950

Richard Mallon was not familiar with sweating on Halloween. No one in Chicago was familiar with sweating on Halloween. The freaky hot weather had turned what is normally a cool fall day into a sweltering hot July-like afternoon. Richard had opened the windows to allow whatever breeze there was to enter the two-bedroom flat and hopefully move some air around and cool the salty-wet back of his neck.

He had risen about an hour earlier and was still feeling the effects of the night before. He had stayed at Henry's Tavern too late as he and Wally celebrated. Their numbers were good for the month, and they had no problems with the collections.

But this morning was payback. The open windows were not working all that well, so plying himself with cold beer would have to suffice for now. He was sitting at the kitchen table, clad in a tee shirt and a pair of boxers. He turned in his chair and tried to reach the refrigerator. His arm was two inches short. Instead of getting up and opening the door of the refrigerator, he yelled out, "Do we have any ice?"

A female voice from another room replied, "In the ice box."

Disappointed that he had to rise from his chair, Richard went to the refrigerator and pulled out a metal ice tray. He took it to the sink where he grabbed a handful of ice cubes, put them in a towel and put it on the back of his neck. He went back to the table and took a long sip from the beer bottle.

Catherine entered the kitchen from Tommy's bedroom. She had a short saber and its decorated leather sheath in her hand. She held it up.

"What is this?" she said to Richard.

"What does it look like?  It's a pirate knife."

"What is this knife doing in our son's bedroom?"

"I heard him say he wanted to be a pirate for Halloween. So, I got it for him from Louie's Pawn Shop. He owed me a favor," Richard said as he rose from the table and took the knife and sheath from Catherine.

"See? Fits real snug," he said as he inserted the knife into the sheath. "This is a beauty. See the detail on the leather? See that?" He held up the sheathed knife for Catherine's inspection. "See that, see that reindeer? That's an art. That's skill." He put the knife on the kitchen table. "Where is he anyway?"

"Wally took him trick-or-treating. You were still asleep when he came home from school," Catherine said as she grabbed the knife and retreated into Tommy's bedroom.

The doorbell rang.

Richard took another sip of beer and looked around the kitchen.

"Do we have anything to give these beggars?" he yelled again to Catherine.

"I told you yesterday to pick something up. Did you?" came the response from the bedroom.

Richard dropped his head. Yes, she did tell him to pick something up. No, he did not. He rose from his chair, went into their bedroom, and put on a pair of pants.

The doorbell rang again.

"Alright, alright," said Richard.

He entered the kitchen and looked around for something to give to the trick-or-treater. There was an apple on the counter. He grabbed it and a knife from the drawer, in the event there was more than one trick-or-treater, he would cut the apple in slices.

He walked down the stairs to answer the door. He opened it and before him stood Wally and Tommy, holding his trick-or-treat bag dressed as a cowboy.

"Pit stop. He's gotta go to the bathroom," said Wally

"Oh," said Richard. He stepped aside to let Wally and Tommy enter the building. Richard stepped out and looked up and down the sidewalk. The block was starting to get crowded with trick-or-treaters. He would soon be barraged with ringing doorbells. He raced inside and up to the apartment where he found Wally sitting on the couch wiping his brow while waiting for Tommy to finish his business.

"God, its hot out there today," said Wally. "They say we may hit ninety today."

"Yeah, it's weird," replied Richard. "Hot as hell."

Tommy came into the living room.

"Hey pal, how's the pickin's so far?"

Tommy opened his bag wide to show Richard.

"Good. Lots of candy. Even have a couple of pennies in there," said Tommy.

"That's great," Richard responded. He took the bag from Tommy, went to the kitchen and dumped the candy into a bowl. He returned the empty bag to Tommy.

"Here you go buddy. Fresh start," he said to Tommy as he handed him back the empty bag.

Catherine came into the room.

"Hello Darling," she said to Tommy.

"Hi mother," said Tommy. "We're going back out again. I just came home to go to the bathroom."

"That's fine," she said.

"Hey," said Richard. "You're dressed as a cowboy! What happened to the pirate?"

"Mom said no to the pirate, so I wore this."

Richard looked at Catherine with a hard stare. She returned same.

Wally saw what was eventually about to erupt and quickly rose from the couch.

"Well, you ready for round two Tommy? Remember we have to swing by and pick up your buddy, what's his name?"

"Freddy Gallagher," said Tommy. "He's my new best friend. He's going to be a devil tonight."

"Yeah, Freddy the Devil. Ooh, sounds scary. Okay, let's go," said Wally as he led Tommy from the apartment.

Richard still held his hard stare. Catherine turned and returned to Tommy's room to continue straightening it out. He followed her and stood in the doorway.

"So why can't he be a pirate? I thought we agreed on this, that a pirate was not as bad as a skeleton or ghost."

Catherine started to make Tommy's bed. "This pagan holiday promotes evil. A pirate is evil."

"Kids dressing up and getting candy is not evil," responded Richard.

"It celebrates the dead. That is not spiritually healthy. The dead have moved on," Catherine said.

"Look, you gotta let this kid be a kid.  He's too young for all this religious nonsense that you're laying on him."

Catherine stopped her work on the bed and turned to Richard. "Religious nonsense?  Is that what it is?"

"Yeah, nonsense!" said Richard.  The heat in the room rose to the next level.

"I am trying to raise a boy on this god forsaken planet according to the wishes of God!  You are not helping!"  She grabbed the sheathed knife and withdrew it for Richard to see.

Realizing that he had set her off, Richard turned to empathy. "I know how you feel.  If I saw a ghost..."

"It was not a ghost!!!" Catherine stated.  "It was the Blessed Mother herself!"

"Okay, not a ghost, the Blessed Mother herself, whatever.  The point is, we can't all be perfect.  Tommy needs to know how the real-world works.  It ain't all hosts and chalices."

"It must be!  I want him to prepare for the priesthood.  I promised the Blessed Mother that I would raise my son to follow her son."

Richard was getting exasperated with this conversation. "Did you tell the Blessed Mother that you would run it by your son's father?  Did that come up in your conversation?"

"He must reject sin!  I have!  And if you want, you can too!"

"Catherine, I'm not going into that shit again," Richard remarked.  "We've talked about this until I'm blue in the face.  You're not Little Miss Sinless!"

Instantly, the brows over Catherine's eyes became knitted.  Still holding the knife, she lunged at Richard and plunged it deep into his chest.  Richard's eyes widened as the red stain on the front of his tee shirt expanded.  He kept his stunned eyes on Catherine as he spoke his last words, "See.  You are a sinner." He smiled and stumbled backwards for a couple of steps and then crumpled to the kitchen floor.

Catherine stared at Richard's body, not in horror, but in a sort of callous curiosity. She tilted her head as if she was looking at a piece of art, trying to make sense of the awkward angles and colors laying on her kitchen floor. She walked to the kitchen counter and grabbed a piece of candy from the bowl of Tommy's early haul. She stepped over the body and entered the front room where she sat until it got dark.

Darkness falls early this time of year. Catherine sat in her darkened living room accompanied by her thoughts and a five-inch-long sheathed knife. She looked at the knife on her lap. The leatherwork on the sheath was intricate. Richard was right about that. She picked the knife up and held it higher so she could closely exam the craftmanship. The reindeer was indeed a piece of art. She raised the sheath to eye level, and she pulled the knife halfway out and stopped when she saw Richard's blood on the blade. Her hand started to shake. She reinserted the knife into the sheath and put it back on her lap.

"God's will," she said to herself.

The doorbell rang.

Catherine rose from the couch and put the knife behind a picture frame that stood on the end table. She descended the stairs of the two-flat building and opened the front door. Wally and cowboy Tommy were standing before her.

"Hi Mom. I got a ton of candy. See!" Tommy opened his bag to show his haul and Catherine feigned interest. She did not fool Wally.

"Everything alright?" Wally inquired.

"Yes, yes. Let's talk about it upstairs."

Catherine led them up the stairs to the apartment, where she shuttled Tommy to his room while shielding his view of the kitchen. Wally's apprehension grew as he stood in the living room and witnessed Catherine's behavior.

After leaving Tommy's bedroom and shutting the door behind her, she entered the living room and calmly said to Wally, "I've killed Richard. He's in the kitchen."

Wally walked to the kitchen where there was a messy pool of blood on the floor and a trail that led to the rear door, where Richard lay, half in and half out of the apartment, apparently lacking the strength or blood supply to continue his attempt to escape out the backdoor before he died. Wally stepped out on to the porch and looked around for peering eyes. Satisfied that there weren't any, he went back into the apartment and dragged Richard by the feet all the way in and closed the door.

Wally went back into the living room, where Catherine stood with the knife and sheath. She handed it to Wally.

"Here. I never want to see this again."

Realizing that he was holding the murder weapon, Wally stuffed the knife in his jacket as he instinctively looked around. He turned back to Catherine.

"What the hell is this?" he said.

"He would not denounce sin."

"Did the Blessed Mother tell you to do this? Did she?"

Catherine's brows knitted again.

"Alright, never mind," said Wally. "Whatever happened, happened." Wally stepped from the living room and went back into the kitchen. He surveyed the surroundings.

"I'm gonna need at least an hour or so to get this cleaned up. It's still early, take Tommy back out while I clean this up."

"I will not take part in this pagan ritual," said Catherine.

"Catherine, you just made a human sacrifice, can you get any more pagan?" Wally calmly explained.

The tone of his voice was respectful and sensical to Catherine. She turned and went to fetch Tommy from his bedroom. Wally placed himself between the view of the kitchen and Tommy's path out the front door as Catherine and her son walked through the front room.

"Bonus candy. Ain't nothing better," said Wally as he waved them out the door.

Wally entered the kitchen and reached under the sink for a bucket and sponge and hopefully some Mr. Clean. As he rose from underneath the sink, he heard a groan. He turned to Richard's body.

Richard was still alive.

Wally went to Richard and knelt next to him on the floor.

"Rich, you there?" said Wally.

Richard slowly blinked his eye and let out a breath in response.

Wally reached into his jacket and pulled out the sheath. He drew the knife and held it next to Richard's chest, just above the original wound.

He talked to Richard in a low, matter-of-fact manner. "I'm sorry buddy. I know she's crazy, but she's family. What are you going to do?"

Wally plunged the knife into Richard. It finished the job.

* * * * * * * *

A little over an hour later, Wally was sitting on the couch in the living room, clad only in his boxers, wife-beater tee shirt and socks. He had a glass of bourbon over ice in his hand which he swirled and took a sip.

"Richie you always bought the cheap stuff," he said aloud to himself.

He took another sip when Catherine and Tommy entered the living room. Tommy was still excited about the bonus trick-or-treat time.

"Uncle Wally, look what I got," Tommy said as he opened his bag to display his latest round of goodies.

"Wow," said Wally. "You made out like a bandit."

"Where are your clothes?" Tommy asked after realizing Wally was sitting in his underwear.

"Oh," said Wally. "I spilt some marinara on them. They're in the bathroom drying."

Catherine looked at Wally. He winked back at her that all was good.

"Okay, go get into your pajamas, Tommy," said Catherine.

"Aw, mom, do I have to go to bed?"

"No," interjected Wally. "We can stay up and watch some television."

"Oh boy!" said Tommy and he scampered off to his room. Catherine quickly moved to block the view of the kitchen from Tommy. She looked into the kitchen and realized it was clean.

Catherine looked at Wally and said, "Well?"

"He's in your bedroom. I had to use your throw rug to roll him up in. And, oh, you're going to need a new shower curtain too. Got kinda messy."

"And then what? I'm not sleeping in that room while he's there."

"I'll take him out later when everybody's home or asleep to a place where he'll be found. They know Rich. They'll chalk it up to business as usual. Just remember, you haven't seen him since he left here earlier today. Got it?"

Catherine nodded.

"Until then, I'll just hang around. I'm also going to need a set of Richie's clothes. Mine are a bit messy. I had to toss them."

Catherine went to her bedroom to get clothes for Wally. She saw the rolled-up carpet laying on the floor in the middle of the room. She stepped over it to the closet and went through Richard's clothing, found a suitable set, and brought them back out to Wally.

"Thanks," said Wally.

The shirt was a silky loose button down that fit Wally despite his body being considerably larger than Richard's. The pants were another matter.

"God, I didn't realize he was so skinny," Wally said as he slid the pants on. He attempted to button the waist but that was impossible. Instead, he zipped them up as high as the zipper would go and let the button remain loose.

"I'm gonna need a belt," Wally said.

For the next two hours Wally and Tommy sat on the couch, eating candy, and catching Uncle Miltie on the Texaco Star Theater. After a couple rounds of laughs, Tommy was fast asleep on the couch.

Catherine, who was in her bedroom kneeling before the roll of carpet and praying, came out to put Tommy to bed.

She asked Wally, "When will you be going?"

"Another hour or two. After midnight," answered Wally as he rose from the couch to pour another drink.

"I will be in my room. Praying for Richard," said Catherine.

"Little late for that, isn't it?" replied Wally.

Catherine remained silent. She went to her bedroom and closed the door.

Wally finished making his drink and went back to the couch. Fireside Theater was just beginning.

When Wally awoke on the couch, it was almost midnight, and it was still hot. He slowly rose and ambled into the kitchen where he splashed some water in his face and mentally prepared for the task he was about to do.

He entered Catherine's bedroom. She was still kneeling over the roll of carpet, with her head down and reciting what Wally assumed were prayers.

"It's time," Wally said. "I'm going to pull the car around."

Catherine turned back to the carpet. She looked at it for a minute, rose and turned to the doorway, stopped, turned again, and kicked the roll of carpet. Then she left the room.

After stashing the sheathed knife safely in the trunk, Wally pulled his 1947 Studebaker Commander around to the alley and parked it directly behind Catherine's apartment. He climbed the two stories up the back porch and entered through the rear door. Catherine was nowhere in sight. Wally realized he would have to do this alone.

He bent over and picked up one end of the carpet roll and dragged it from the bedroom to the back door. He paused. Breathing heavily, he wiped his brow with a handkerchief. After he checked for prying eyes, he dragged the roll outside and along the porch to the stairs that wound down two stories to the backyard. He pulled the roll down the stairs, each stair causing a muffled bump, until he got to the bottom of the stairway where he dragged the carpet roll to the yard.

He stopped again and took another break. As he bent over with his hands on his knees, he took several heavy breaths, stood up, pulled out a pack of Lucky Strikes and lit a cigarette. He leaned against the fence as he took his first drag and looked into the night sky.

It was a clear night. Wally thought for a moment that Richard might already be up there in the heavens, looking down at him dragging his body.

He laughed to himself as he exhaled smoke into the heavens. After another drag, he flicked the cigarette into the next yard and turned back to the carpet roll.

"Okay buddy, time to go," he said as he lifted the end of the carpet roll and dragged it through the yard and into the alley to his car. He put Richie down as he opened the trunk. He tried to lift the top portion of the body into the trunk, but he got it halfway before his strength gave out and he collapsed to the ground with the dead weight of the body and carpet falling on him.

Wally was wedged under his car, with the carpet roll pining him in.  He lay on his side, with his right arm trapped beneath him and the carpet preventing him from moving his left arm.  He tried to wiggle himself loose.  His frustration turned his wiggle into a violent shaking that resulted in his making the situation worse as rust bits and specks of dirt fell into his face from the undercarriage of the car.  He tried to spit out the bits that fell into his mouth, but the rapid spitting turned into a vocal "Fuck!"

Wally was trapped beneath the car and body of his one-time best friend, contemplating his next move when he heard a voice.

"Need some help?"

He turned his head a fraction and saw the face of the Devil just behind the driver's side rear wheel.

"Need some help?" said the Devil repeating his offer.

Wally teetered between fear and disbelief as he let out a squeaky "Yes."

The Devil took its mask off.  It was Freddy Gallagher.  He was still in his Halloween costume.  Wally was relieved.  He was in no spiritual shape right now to have a face-to-face with the Devil.

"Freddy, Freddy," said Wally, "Can you roll that carpeting off me?"

"Yeah, sure," said Freddy.  Ten seconds later, Freddy, using his leverage, had successfully rolled the carpet roll off Wally, who crawled out from underneath the car and sat on the edge of the trunk.

"What are you doing?" said Freddy, with his mask on top of his head.

"Oh nothing," said Wally.

"Then what's this?" said Freddy, pointing at the roll of carpet.

"Old carpet.  I'm getting rid of it for Mrs. Mallon."

"At this time of night?" continued Freddy.

"Yeah, it's easier to get rid of.  Speaking of time of night, what are you doing out?"

"I couldn't sleep."

"Do your parents know that you're out?"

"Hell no.  They are both passed out on the couch," Freddy said.

"Well, help me get this carpet in the trunk and I'll give you five bucks," said Wally.  "But you have to go right home after.  Okay?"

"Six.  Six bucks.  And a buck for helping you get out from beneath the car.  That's seven.  Seven bucks," said Freddy.

"You know, for a delinquent you have pretty good math skills.  Alright, seven it is.  Grab that end of the carpet."  Wally pointed to the end where the feet are, the lighter load.  He grabbed the opposite end Freddy did not move.

"You helping me or not?  Grab that end."

"I need payment upfront," said Freddy.

Wally put his end down and reached into his pocket and pulled out some cash.

"I've got two fives.  You have any change?"

Freddy shook his head.  "I can give you some candy if you want."

"No," said Freddy.  "Here's ten.  Now let's get this thing going."

Freddy bent over and grabbed his end of the carpet.

Wally counted off, "one, two, three," and they successfully lifted the carpet roll into the trunk.  Wally turned and saw a pair of headlights a couple of blocks down.  He had no idea who they were, but he was not taking any chances.  He quickly got into the driver's seat and started the car.

"Close the trunk, Freddy.  I gotta go."

Freddy obeyed.  The trunk lid shut, and Wally drove off.

Wally took Ashland north, just past 35th Street and pulled onto a gravel sideroad that led to the branch of the Chicago River known as Bubbly Creek.  Whatever could not be used from butchered hogs and cows in the Union Stock Yards was tossed into the creek to decompose, and hence, its name. A human body floating amid the little blasts of carbon dioxide would surely be noticed. In time.

Wally backed the car to the edge of the creek, popped the trunk and out popped the Devil.

"What the fuck!" cried a terrified Wally as he stumbled backwards and fell into the creek.

The Devil started to laugh.

"Boo," said the Devil as he took his mask off.

A dripping wet Wally rose from the water. "You little shit!" He started to walk out of the water and by the time he got to the bank of the creek, he was also laughing.

"Okay, you got me. Let's get this thing in the river and get out of here."

Like a pair of deckhands who routinely move loads of goods, they removed the carpet roll.

"On three,' said Wally. Freddy nodded. They swung the carpet roll back and forth to develop momentum, and then Wally started the count.

"One."

"Two."

"Three!"

At the same instant, both Freddy and Wally released their ends of the carpet and tossed it about ten feet into the creek, enough for it to float away towards 39th Street. Wally smiled as he watched the results of the united effort. He turned to Freddy who was holding one of Richard's shoes.

Wally grabbed the shoe from Freddy and threw it as far as he could into the creek.

"I've been looking for that shoe," said Wally. "Threw the other one out when I couldn't find it. C'mon, let's go get some fried shrimp."

Wally drove them to the 26th Street Shrimp Shack.  It was open twenty-four hours and was a regular stop for Wally.  The Shrimp Shack was a small building that stood by itself on the east side of Ashland, next to the Chicago River.  The riverfront location gave the Shack a seafood credibility even though anything caught in the river was inedible.

Wally went into the Shack and brought back two pounds of shrimp and a cup of sauce.  He placed the feast between them in the front seat and opened the containers.

"Dig in," Wally said as he grabbed a big shrimp and dipped it into the cup of sauce.

Freddy watched Wally eat the piece of shrimp.

"C'mon, dig in," said Wally.  "This is good stuff."

Freddy obeyed, took a shrimp from the bag and dipped into the sauce.  He bit into it, chewed, and made his pronouncement.

"Whoa, this IS good," said Freddy.

"Did you ever have shrimp before?" said Wally.

"No. We don't go out to eat much."

"That's too bad.  You miss out on a lot of good stuff."

Freddy finished his piece of shrimp and reached for another.

"So, what do you do?  Are you a junkman or something?"

"Yeah," said Wally.  "I guess you could say that."

"Good money?" continued Freddy.

"Yeah.  Enough anyway."

"Cool.  I think I may want to be a junkman when I grow up."

"You may want to set your sights a little higher, Freddy."

"But this was cool.  You ran from the cops, got rid of some garbage, and get to eat fried shrimp," Freddy said as he reached for another shrimp.

"It ain't all it's cracked up to be, believe me.  And we aren't sure if that car in the alley were cops.  Time to go home."

Wally wiped his hands with a napkin, then wiped them on his pants for good measure, and drove out of the parking lot and on to Ashland, this time heading south.

Wally pulled over in front of Freddy's apartment building, which was two blocks away from Catherine's apartment.

"Okay, Freddy. Your parents are probably worried sick about you."

"Uh, I doubt it. See you later Wally."

Freddy exited the car and walked through the gangway to the rear of the apartment building, walked up the porch steps to the kitchen window of the apartment, slid it open and climbed in. He quietly entered the kitchen and closed the window behind him. He tip-toed past the living room where his parents were still on the couch just as he had left them, and into his bedroom.

He sat on his bed and took his devil costume off, rolled it up and threw it to the corner of the room. He rose from the bed and reached into his pants pocket. He pulled out the knife and sheath that he had found in Wally's trunk.

He looked at it and marveled at the reindeer on the handle. He then put it into his dresser drawer and went to bed.

# CHAPTER 12

# THE WEEK BEFORE CHRISTMAS 1970

Weezer entered the confessional, knelt, and made the sign of the cross aloud. "In the name of the Father, the Son, and the Holy Ghost. Bless me Father, for I have sinned. It has been...," he paused as he tried to recall the last time he was in confession at St. Justin, "...three weeks since my last confession."

He knew it was longer than that. Much longer. Then he wondered if lying while confessing your sins would blow the whole thing. Why chance it?

"Father, can I start again?" he asked.

The silhouette on the other side of the confessional screen nodded and said, "Yes, sure."

"Thank you. Bless me Father, no. In the name of the Father, the Son, and the Holy Ghost. Bless me Father, for I have sinned. It has been four months since my last confession." Weezer paused again, waiting for any blowback he had coming.

"Continue," said the priest.

"I have lied three times, I hit a kid in the schoolyard, but he kind of deserved it, and swore five, no, six times. Seven. I am sorry for these and all my sins."

The voice behind the screen recited his absolution of Weezer's sins in a quick and rote manner, like a commercial announcer trying to get the fine print into the end of a radio ad. "May our Lord and God, Jesus Christ, through the grace and mercies of his love for humankind, forgive you all your transgressions. And I, by His power given me, forgive and absolve you from all your sins, in the name of the Father and of the Son and of the Holy Spirit."

Still not feeling totally absolved for what bothered him, Weezer opened the door to the confessional and stepped out. The next person in line, an elderly woman who was clutching her rosaries, stepped to the box. Weezer turned and walked back into the confessional. He popped his head out and said to the woman, "Sorry. Forgot about one," and ducked back into the confessional.

"Father, it's me again."

"You?" said the priest behind the screen.

"Yeah, Father, I had a question."

"Okay."

"Father, what if you didn't commit a sin, but felt like you did."

"What do you mean?"

"I mean, Father, what happens when something happens to someone, but you weren't there, but maybe the person who had something happen to them maybe wouldn't have something happen to them because they were thinking about something that they should not have done earlier in the day. Should I have confessed it to you?"

After a slight chuckle, the priest said, "I'm not quite sure of what you just said, but you said that you didn't commit a sin. What makes you say that?"

"Well Father, I wasn't there.  I didn't do anything, but I just can't help feeling guilty about it."

"Feeling guilty about something does not mean it's a sin."

"You mean like, guilt and sin aren't the same thing?"

The priest paused.  "Okay, suppose I'm on a diet.  Trying to lose a couple of pounds.  I see some cookies laying on a plate in the kitchen.  I eat one and start to walk away.  You with me so far?"

"Yes Father.  I'm listening."

"But I stop, turn around and grab a second cookie and eat it. After I eat it, I feel guilty that I strayed from my diet.  Is that a sin?"

"Were the cookies yours?"

"What?  Why do you ask that?"

"Well, if they weren't, and you took them, that would be stealing.  That's a sin, right?"

"No, no.  I was allowed to eat the cookies."

"Well, if you didn't swipe the cookies, I guess it wasn't a sin.  But you said you still felt guilty."

"Yes, I did," continued the priest.  "Sometimes you realize you didn't need cookies or, apple pies."

Weezer noticed a shift in the priest's voice and was expecting some sort of bad news.

The priest continued speaking in a deliberate and measured manner.  "Guilt is something that you work out with yourself.  Sin you work out with God.  That's why you are here today, to confess your sins to God and seek his absolution through an act of penance. The guilt that you feel.  That is something that you must work out with yourself.  Ask yourself some questions.  Why do I feel guilty? Could I have done something different?  Would it have changed anything?"

The priest paused.  "You ask yourself; did I make the right decision?"

Weezer could not decide as to whether he should answer the priest's rhetorical question, so he didn't. He felt uncomfortable in more ways than one as he shifted the weight on his knees by gently rocking side-ways on the leather covered kneeling pads. The sound of rippling leather brought the priest back to the more important issue of the moment, Weezer's spiritual well-being.

"There is no need for penance or absolution from me. Sometimes it's just God's will and you will have to let it be at that. Do you understand?"

"Yes Father. But I still feel this guilt in my gut."

"The penance you do will help."

"Well, if you say so. Penance."

Weezer rose again from the kneeler and opened the door to find the line waiting for absolution had doubled in length. The elderly woman at the head of the line approached the entry and glared at Weezer, as did most of the line. Feeling the bad energy from the waiting sinners, Weezer turned to them and said, "I had a fun week. Alright?" and walked out from the church.

"Guilt ain't sin, guilt ain't sin," Weezer said to himself amid the scattering of snowflakes that were whirling about like they had somewhere to go. He walked home like he was on some sort of autopilot. All he could think about was "Guilt ain't sin." When he got home, he was still trying to make heads or tails of what Father Mallon was trying to sell him. Penance? Penance is just saying five Hail Mary's and a couple of Our Fathers and you're good to go until the next time. The recital of some well-worn prayers can fix your sins, but it can't do anything about your guilt.

Pizza was waiting on the kitchen table along with the paper plates. He walked into the living room and found his mother sitting on the couch, amid the boxes of Christmas ornaments and decorations brought down from the attic by Weezer's father before he left for his tree-selling shift.  She did not look happy as she smoked her Virginia Slim and watched the television.

"Is Dad home yet?"

"Not yet," she said as she checked her watch.  "He was due home a half hour ago.  We'll give him fifteen minutes.  If he isn't home by then, to hell with him."

Just then, Weezer's father appeared at the back door, carrying the Christmas tree, moderately sober and hungry.  "Sorry for the delay, dear.  Is the pizza still hot?"

"Hot enough," said Weezer's mother as she stubbed out her cigarette.

Weezer's father dragged the tree through the house to the front room and stood it up for everyone to see.

"Well?" said Weezer's father.

"It's nice dear.  Come and eat," said Weezer's mother from the kitchen.

Weezer followed his father into the front room and scanned the tree up and down.  "Turn it around a little," Weezer said.

His father turned the tree halfway around for Weezer's perusal.

"That's better," said Weezer.  "It's kind of thin on the other side. We can put that side against the windows."

Weezer's father nodded. His mother yelled from the kitchen, "C'mon and eat!  Now!"

Weezer grabbed the stand and set it beneath the tree while his father placed the trunk into it.  Weezer tightened the bolts of the stand that kept the tree erect and his father let go.  The tree stood by itself with a slight tilt to the right.

"It's okay," said Weezer's father.  "We can just turn it a bit towards the windows.  It'll be fine.  I'll get us some pizza and some water for the tree."

Weezer stood up and gave the tree another look-over and turned it, stood back and nodded.

"Looks good," he said to himself. He opened a box of decorations and explored the contents.

In the kitchen, Weezer's mother turned to his father, "You're surprisingly sober tonight."

His father nodded. "We sold a lot of trees tonight. I was too busy to get loaded, believe it or not. But I'll work on that later."

"Oh goody," said his mother.

Weezer's father took a piece of square-cut pizza and crammed it into his mouth then filled a large glass of water from the sink to pour into the tree stand.

"Hm, pizza's good," he mumbled while chewing. He swallowed and then said, more clearly to his wife, "Do we have any sugar?"

"For what?" she said.

"I heard today that if you put some sugar into the water, it acts like a plant food. It's good for the tree."

"It's in the pantry where it's been for the past twenty-five years. Knock yourself out," said Weezer's mother.

Weezer's father found his sugar, added a heaping tablespoon to the water and shook the glass to mix it. "This should work," he said as he grabbed the plate of pizza with his free hand and went to the living room.

Weezer had just finished plugging in the tree lights, when his father walked in, hands full of pizza and sugar water. Without any ornaments to distract from their brilliance, the red, blue, green, and yellow bulbs seemed brighter and even more joyous.

"Turn 'em off," said Weezer's father.

"But Dad."

"Turn 'em off. Turn 'em off now. Don't argue with me."

Weezer obeyed and unplugged the cord from the outlet. He took a seat on the couch.

With the tree lights out, the background of windows, shades, sills and a Gold Star Banner stood out more prominently.

"That's better," said Weezer's father.  He put the pizza and water down on the coffee table and walked to the front window where the gold star banner hung by a thin rope from the window latch.  He took the banner and hung it from the next window, where it could still be seen from indoors.

"I was going to do that," said Weezer.

After he rehung the banner, Weezer's father wiped a tear from the corner of his eye and then said, "Let's hang some ornaments, shall we?"

The spirit and enthusiasm Weezer had felt were now miles away, gone to wherever lost expectations and ruined anticipations go to morph into huge disappointments and permeate the atmosphere of the moment.

Weezer slowly rose from the couch as if he was about to do a household chore rather than participate in a special holiday family event.  Sensing Weezer's mood, his father tried, again, to explain his aversion to Christmas tree lights.

"I'm sorry about the lights," said Weezer's father.  "But you knew about this.  About me.  I'm sorry son, I just can't take it.  This symbol of joy and good-will illuminating the banner in the window.  Greg's banner."

"I know, Dad.  It's just, you know," Weezer softly said after he rose from the couch.

"No, I don't know.  Tell me."

After a deep breath, Weezer replied, "You gotta get over this Dad."

"Get over it?"

"The crying, the feeling bad. It's been almost three years.  We've got to move on, all of us," said Weezer.  He gestured to his mother as she walked into the room.

Weezer's father became defensive.  "Okay, Mr. Big-Shot.  You gonna tell me how I feel?  What do you know?"

"I know what I see every day. We live under the same roof, remember?" said Weezer. "Or does that slip your mind sometimes?"

Weezer's father raised his right hand but was grabbed by his wife. He looked at her and slowly dropped his arm. He turned to leave and announced that he was "going to help Fat Billy close the tree lot," which meant he would be back in a couple of hours in an intoxicated condition.

Weezer and his mother looked at each other, shrugged and gave the 'what are you going to do' look. Weezer's mother pulled out a shiny red ornament. She turned and hung it on the tree.

"C'mon," she said to Weezer. "You and I."

Weezer then grabbed another ornament from the box, a plastic reindeer, and hung it on the opposite side of the tree.

The contents of the ornament box were reduced to old tree needles and loose hangers. Weezer's mother stepped back and looked at the tree. She reached into the pocket of her apron and pulled out her pack of Virginia Slims, and matches. She lit it and inhaled the long, thin cigarette while she raised her chin as she let out the smoke.

"Beautiful," she said. "With or without lights."

Weezer looked at the tree from her angle and agreed to a certain extent.

"Yeah, beautiful," he said, "but it would be more beautiful with lights."

* * * * * * * *

Father Cummins entered the study of the rectory with a glass of scotch in hand, and found Father Mallon and Father Burke, sitting in front of the fireplace in matching padded wing chairs, with a small table between them. The table had a stack of books piled on it. Father Mallon was holding a hunting knife while Father Burke had a book on his lap and was softly sobbing.

"What is it this time?" thought Father Cummins.

"Is that something I need to worry about?" said Father Cummins as he pointed to the sheathed knife that Father Mallon was inspecting.

"God, no," said Father Mallon, "I'm too tired to commit any murder tonight. Just don't tick me off tomorrow."

"And you," said Father Cummins as he turned to Father Burke. "What are you weeping about? You look like a little girl."

Father Burke smiled and wiped his eyes. "You're right. I do look like a little girl. I can't help it. I just finished *Love Story*."

"You mean that overly sentimental piece of rubbish that romanticizes dying from a horrible, painful, disease that is the number one best seller in the country?" replied Father Cummins.

"Yes, that's the one," said Father Burke. "The library finally had a copy for me. I'm sure I can get a homily or two out of it. Would you like to read it before I return it?"

"Hard pass. No thank you."

"Well, I'll just leave it here if you change your mind. I've got to go up and call my mother. It's Saturday night you know," said Father Burke as he placed the book on the table and rose from the chair.

"Good night, Father Burke," said Father Cummins as he eyed the chair where Father Burke had been sitting. He paused and turned to Father Mallon before he sat down.

"Do you mind if I join you?" he said.

"Welcome," said Father Mallon as he gestured for Father Cummins to sit.

Father Cummins settled into the chair and sipped the scotch he had brought. "Nice fire," he said.

"Yes, it is cozy," said Father Mallon. "It certainly helps when one is doing a bit of reflecting."

"Reflecting, are we?" said Father Cummins.

"Like a damn mirror," said Father Mallon gazing at the fire.

"I thought I would do some reading before bed. Fires are also very good for reading. And I'll read silently. I promise," said Father Cummins.

Father Mallon smiled and took a sip of his own tumbler of scotch.

"Is there a reason that you're so tired?" asked Father Cummins.

"Sleep has been hard to come by lately. I don't know why," said Father Mallon. "Well, I guess I do."

"Thinking of Freddy again?" asked Father Cummins.

"Yeah, lately. I have."

"I guess my wise words didn't help."

"Yes, they did. I felt at peace with myself after we spoke," said Father Mallon while still inspecting the knife in his hand. He put the knife on the table between the two chairs and turned to Father Cummins. "I know that I was not responsible for his death, you helped me get over that. But there's this leftover, detritus of guilt."

"There should be no guilt. You helped vanquish the devil himself." Father Cummins paused, as if he was debating with himself, before he continued, "The world is a better place without Freddy Gallagher. Believe me."

Father Mallon felt that Father Cummins attitude towards Freddy was a bit odd, as if he knew something about Freddy that Father Mallon was not aware of.

"Why so rough on Freddy?" asked Father Mallon.

"Let's just say he wasn't just a wayward lad, he was downright evil."

"But you thought he was salvageable. You told me yourself."

"Yeah, I think everyone is salvageable. That may be a fault of mine." Father Cummins paused. "It's probably why I became a priest."

"You mean that you wanted to salvage people?"

"No, I meant the fault part. I'm human," Father Cummins said as he sipped from his drink.

A smiling Father Mallon replied, "Ah, the human card. It's nice to have that in your back pocket every now and then."

"It's certainly convenient, but also accurate. People look at us as some sort of conduit to God. And I suppose that's correct to a certain extent. They believe that they are talking with God when they reveal their sins to us in the confessional, and if they believe it, then it's true."

Father Cummins rose from the chair and grabbed a log from a pile that lay next to the fireplace. He tossed the log into the fire and stoked it, energizing the flames.

"But see, the problems come when they are listening to you, thinking that this conduit is a two-way deal, that God not only hears you through us, which is true, but whatever you say is coming from God," Father Cummins said looking into Father Mallon's eyes.

"That's screwed up. If God is speaking to them through us, his message is being filtered through the human element, which, on any given day, means that it's probably more wrong than right. That's where the human card comes in handy. When your advice turns out to be shit, you pull out the human card and let it be at that."

"I thought it was only me."

"Oh, hell no," said Father Cummins. "It's very common. Our Faith is based on being human, striving for divine forgiveness. Every-one who walks into the confessional plays the human card, and then walks out with a clean slate, free to be human for another week."

Father Mallon took another drink from his tumbler and picked up the knife. He stared at it as he switched it between his hands.

"I'm going to go out on a limb here and guess that knife has something to do with Freddy," said Father Cummins. "Am I right?"

Father Mallon smiled and nodded, "Yes, yes it does. He gave me this on my sixteenth birthday. It was the last birthday present I ever received. From anyone." He looked up at Father Cummins and handed the knife to him. "Here. Take a look, it's definitely a unique piece."

Father Cummins accepted the knife and pulled the six-inch blade from the beautifully beaded cover. His eyes became fixed on the reindeer that was exquisitely carved into the handle.

"You say Freddy gave you this on your sixteenth birthday?"

"Yeah."

Father Cummins looked up. "What was that fifty-six?"

"Yeah, May of 1956. Why?"

"Oh, nothing. Just figuring out maybe when or where it was made. You're right, it is unique. This reminds you of Freddy? Why this?"

Father Mallon had previously asked himself the same question, but he decided that the bowling ball he had would have been too unwieldly laying in his lap while reminiscing of Freddy. Especially while he was drinking. In addition, the dried blood that turned the GO'D imprint on the ball from white to dark crimson was perhaps a bit too ghoulish.

"It's the only thing he ever gave me, other than a life-changing tip at the racetrack, which I told you of before."

Father Cummins nodded his head.

"But the knife kind of symbolizes when he became a permanent fixture in my life."

"How so?" asked Father Cummins.

"Well, Wally immediately made him an earner after that. He became part of us. It was kind of random, but I have always connected the two together. The timing and everything."

"Yeah, probably," said Father Cummins. "The timing."

A pause lingered over the room.

"Well enough of this. I'm going to bed," said Father Mallon. He rose from the chair. "Good night, Father Cummins."

"Good night, Tom. I'm going to have another drink and read some of the Good Book," said Father Cummins holding up a Bible that was laying amid other books on the side table next to his chair.

"I hear everyone dies in the end," said Father Mallon.

Father Cummins laughed, "Yeah, but I heard the reviews were pretty good."

"Good night, Father Cummins. See you in the morning."

Father Mallon entered his room and went to the closet, where he took out his dark bag and placed it on the bed. He sat next to it and uncovered the contents; the bowling ball and the lug nut Freddy had given him. He also stored the knife in there. The bag contained the mysteries of his life. He had an explanation for all the items but lacked the 'why.' Why were these items so mysterious and more importantly, why were they in his life at all?

The first year at the parish where he grew up had brought back memories, regrets, and hints at dark secrets that he knew existed but for whatever reason, he did not want to know. There was some sort of symbiotic relationship between the dormant, inert items, that he knew. A karma that he could not figure out, yet he knew it involved both of his parents, Uncle Wally, Freddy, and the path he chose for his life. And maybe God himself.

He could not just leave it at that.

He put the mystery items back into the closet, undressed and crawled under the blankets. He stared into the dark. He turned under the blankets and closed his eyes. Then opened them again. He continued the routine twice more before the scotch helped to put him in a state where his body could rest. The dreams and images to come in the night would be another matter.

Father Cummins sat back in his chair. He took a sip of the scotch and placed the glass on the table next to him. With the open Bible on his lap, he strained to hear Father Mallon walk up the squeaky staircase to the upstairs sleeping area. After determining that Father

Mallon's ascent was complete, he closed the Bible and put it back on the table. He grabbed another book from the short stack on the table and opened it to the page where he had left off a couple days earlier. He had started *Love Story* the week before and was nearing the end. He anticipated finishing the book that evening.

He started reading, but after one paragraph he gave up and closed the book.

Father Cummins' mind could not leave the bedside of a mortally wounded Wally at Holy Cross Hospital.

Wally had requested Father Cummins' attendance at the hospital. There were not a lot of people that Wally could call to be with him in his final hours. Tommy was off at the seminary and Freddy was in jail. He was sure that if he called anyone else, they would come up with an excuse or just flat-out not come after saying that they would be there.

Plus, he had something to tell Father Cummins.

When Father Cummins arrived at Wally's hospital room, he found Wally in bed, attached to the various tubes and devices, and clutching a rosary. His eyes stared at the ceiling as his lips moved in sync to the prayers he recited on each bead of the rosary. Father Cummins glanced at the orderly that stood next to Wally. The orderly glanced back and slowly shook his head.

Father Cummins bent over and spoke to Wally.

"Wally. Wally. This is Father Cummins. I'm here."

Wally turned his head and smiled. In a slow and weak voice, he said, "Thanks for coming Father." A small cough interrupted him. "Get closer so I can talk to God."

Father Cummins got closer and then, slowly, Wally confessed his sins to the priest who strained to catch the raspy words of the dying confessor. He nodded his head as Wally struggled to say what he had to say. Knowing that time was of the essence, he did not ask Wally to repeat anything as he deciphered the words upon hearing them.

Father Cummins gave the prayer of absolution and made the sign of the cross over Wally.

Wally then passed away. But not before confessing to Father Cummins that he and Catherine had used "the Reindeer" on Richard, and "that stupid fucking kid Freddy" was holding on to the "Reindeer," a term that Father Cummins did not understand until tonight.

Father Cummins took another sip of his drink. The Seal of Confession prevented him from telling any of this to Father Mallon. He had to let it be at that.

* * * * * * *

Next to the Sunday paper, the Thursday edition of the *Chicago Today* was the thickest of the week and therefore the least susceptible to the windy conditions that existed on Christmas Eve. The temperature was in the mid-twenties. The wind shaved a couple of degrees from the temperature but created atmospheric conditions that had to be reckoned with when throwing a rolled-up ink-stained informational projectile from your bicycle to the front porch of a home. Thursday's paper, however, had the heft needed to cut through the air without much timing or anticipation.

Weezer, an experienced thrower, routinely finished his route. He pulled onto the sidewalk and stopped at the corner of 71$^{st}$ and Damen. The sun was dying behind the dark winter clouds that reminded Weezer of the lights on the Christmas tree at his house.

He was at the intersection where Sean O'Brien was hit by the car. He had heard that Sean had crossed against the light as if he was thinking about something else.

Weezer stared at the street and envisioned Sean lying motionless. In his mind's eye, he saw Sean get up and turn to the curb and back again to face the street. The traffic continued as if nothing happened.  Sean attempted to cross the street and this time is hit by a different car.  The other cars in the street stopped as Sean again rose and walked to the curb.  The cars continued.  Sean walked into the intersection and is struck by a Chicago Tribune newspaper panel truck.

This deadly routine continued three more times before Weezer shook his head and came back to reality.  It occurred to him that Sean had been hit by a car four times prior to his deadly accident.

Maybe this was inevitable, thought Weezer.  Maybe the fifth time was just the charm for Sean and had nothing to do with Weezer or his sins.  Maybe.

Weezer left the intersection and headed for home.  He had one more thing to accomplish that evening.

He parked his bike in the yard and hurried into the house.  As he entered the rear door, he called out, "Ma, where's the wrapping paper?  And tape?"  Noticing that she was not in the kitchen, he continued into the living room where his parents sat in their chairs, watching television.

The lights on the Christmas tree were lit.

"Ma, ...," said Weezer.  He stopped when he noticed the lights on the tree.  He turned to his father who sat in his leather chair in the corner, sucking on a Camel and watching Fahey Flynn deliver the early newscast.

"Lights," was all that Weezer could utter.  His father turned and looked at him like he was expecting more words to come from Weezer's mouth.  He realized that his father was accommodating him.  Silent victories are good, he thought.

He turned back to his mother.  "Ma, where's the wrapping paper?"

"In the hall closet, honey.  Do you like the lights?"  She smiled at him.

"Yeah, Ma. They're beautiful." He gave a knowing smile. "But I have to wrap some stuff. I'll be in the basement." He turned to leave the room, stopped and turned back to his father: "Thanks Dad."

Weezer's father raised his right hand, smiled, and said, "Merry Christmas."

Weezer left the room, gathered the wrapping paper and went into the basement. Fifteen minutes later, he left the house through the basement door and put three wrapped boxes into the paper bag on his handlebars.

He pedaled into the cold wind for three blocks to the Fletcher household on 72nd Street and Wolcott. The widow Fletcher lived in the home with her three grade-school children.

Weezer parked his bike and took the wrapped gift boxes from his bag, brought them up to the porch and put them next to the front door. He rang the doorbell, ran down the stairs, jumped on his bike and rode it to a large bush across the street from the Fletcher's house. He watched as the porch light came on and the front door opened. Mrs. Fletcher stepped out, dressed in a holiday dress, holding a martini glass. A man who was also dressed for the holidays came out behind her. Mrs. Fletcher saw the gifts on the porch and cried, "I don't need any fucking charity!" as she kicked one of the boxes off the porch and down the stairs. The wrapping paper flew off the box which revealed a Chrissy Doll, With the Hair That Grows.

The man who came out with her took hold of Mrs. Fletcher and said, "Hey, hey. They're only trying to be nice. Let's see who they're from." He bent over and picked up one of the packages and read aloud the gift tag. "From Santa Claus," he said. He looked up and down the block, saw nothing and turned to Mrs. Fletcher.

"Come on, let's go inside. The girls will love these." They went back into the house and turned off the light.

Weezer waited a couple of minutes before he emerged from behind the bush.  He shook his head and said to himself, "Just gotta let it be at that." He then jumped on his bike and went home.

## THE END

# ACKNOWLEDGEMENTS

The writing of this book was done with the help of a lot of friends. My cousin, Dan Byrne was the first person that I asked to read my work. I asked him over the phone so I could not tell if he rolled his eyes or not, but I doubt if he did. John Linehan also gave me some advice on the book and dealing with Amazon.

Other readers were Dennis Bingham, Antoine McKay and Gary Washburn. Thanks guys. Beers are coming.

Thanks to Sharon Martig for sharing Jim Elsener's post regarding his editing skills. Thank you, Jim, for practicing those skills on this book. Adverbs suck.

And finally, my family. My IT guy was my daughter Lucy and Grace was my graphic arts pro. You kids are amazing! And Laura, my beautiful wife. She faithfully read whatever I gave her did not hesitate to point out what she did nor didn't like. Thank you baby.

Bob Allen is a life-long resident of Chicago, mostly on the south side. He is the proud father of two beautiful girls, Lucy and Grace, with his lovely wife, Laura. The beautiful girls have left he and Laura alone with two rescue cats who let them live with them.

Bob's past involves making eyeglasses, stand-up comedy, loading airplanes, practicing law, and tending bar, among other things. His play, "Opening Day" was produced to exactly zero reviews, however a friend gave it four stars on the way out, so there's that. Also, just in case you were wondering, Bob likes the Sox over the Cubs, thin crust over deep dish, dry over wet, Stones over the Beatles and Ginger over Mary Ann.

Contact Bob at AuthorBobAllen.com